UNCLE ZACH

BEY DECKARD

CONTENTS

Copyright 2023 Bey Deckard
Published by Bey Deckard
All rights reserved

ISBN: 978-1-989250-19-8

This book is sold subject to the condition that it shall not, by way of trade or otherwise, be lent, resold, hired out or otherwise circulated without the publisher's prior consent in any form of binding or cover other than that in which it is published and without a similar condition including this condition being imposed on the subsequent purchaser.

The author does not consent to any Artificial Intelligence (AI), generative AI, large language model, machine learning, chatbot, or other automated analysis, generative process, or replication program to reproduce, mimic, remix, summarize, or otherwise replicate any part of this creative work, via any means: print, graphic, sculpture, multimedia, audio, or other medium. No part of this book has been created using AI-generated images or narrative.

AUTHOR'S NOTE

So, here's 40k of shameless smut. It's just porn, really. Obviously, I had to get it out of my system before tackling something more serious. 😅

I just want to mention here that *in Owen and Zach's fictional world, there are no STIs*. None.

Like, if you asked Zach why he doesn't wear a condom with Owen, despite Owen never refusing a stranger's load, Zach would laugh and say:

"Why would I wear a condom? It's not like I can *actually* get the little slut pregnant."

Anyway, enjoy—and please read the CWs!

THEMES & CONTENT WARNINGS

This story contains: incest, dirty talk (including use of female terms for male anatomy), bareback, cum fetish, D/s, sadomasochism, rape play, toys, gangbang, free use, piss play, prostate milking, somnophilia, dacryphilia, e-stim, voyeurism/exhibitionism, humiliation, ownership tattoo, orgasm denial/forced orgasm, cockwarming, medical play, enema/colonic, large insertions, gapes, male lingerie, and DP.

This is a book of pure fantasy, and the characters are all over 18.

ONE
NO LOAD REFUSED

I FINISHED MY CLEANSE, threw on my lucky sky-blue jockstrap, and lay facedown on the bed, a pillow wedged under my hips. After making myself comfortable, I changed my status to "westside inn rm 203 open door 💦🍑 no load refused" and watched some porn on my phone while I waited.

The first guy showed up about twenty minutes later. He was super quiet and seemed nervous as he crossed the hotel room to the bed where I lay waiting, ass up and ready for him. I watched him out of the corner of my eye as he lubed up his cock. Not bad looking —a little dishevelled, but in a cute sort of way.

He quickly sunk his dick into my hole and let out such a loud groan that I thought for a sec that he'd already blown his load. But then he started fucking me with these fast little thrusts, and I smiled, burying my face in the pillow. His dick was on the small side, which was fine with me—it was an excellent way to warm up for what I hoped would be a full evening. The last time I'd done an "open door," eleven guys had bred me before I'd closed up shop for the night. I was crossing my fingers that I'd break that record tonight.

I could tell Nervous Guy was starting to get close, but right then, the door hinges creaked, heralding my second visitor of the night. Unfortunately, his arrival spooked the first guy. He pulled out without giving me a load and left, almost tripping over himself in his hurry to flee the scene.

Ah well.

The new guy was a big beefy dude who was probably in his late fifties. He didn't bother with lube; he just went old school and spat in his hand before feeding his cock slowly into my hole, then proceeded to fuck the hell out of me. I grunted as he pounded my ass, savouring every deep thrust of his girthy cock, then moaned in encouragement as he sped up, greedy for him to fill me with his cum. Beefy Dude gasped as he hammered his dick into me, his big hands around my hips, jerking me back against him, then flooded my hole with a few deep thrusts. Afterwards, he patted my ass cheek in a friendly way, and I sighed happily.

After he left, I didn't have long to wait. I had three more guys pay me a visit in quick succession, leaving my ass a creamy, dripping mess. Afterwards, there was a lull, so I watched more porn, hoping that wasn't it for the night.

Number six arrived just as I was starting to lose hope. He had some trouble staying hard, but in the end, he managed to leave a deposit.

After he was gone, I helped myself to a little bottle of vodka from the minifridge, then settled back on the bed to wait for my next guests. Finally, around ten-thirty, it began to pick up, with sometimes two guys waiting on the sidelines for their turns. I lay there in bliss, my face buried in the pillow as one guy after another worked my ass until my hole was loose and sloppy and throbbing in the most delicious way.

I started to get a little sleepy as the clock crept toward midnight, and my ass was starting to get tender. I was *really* looking forward to pushing out all those loads to jack off with—maybe it was time to call it a night?

The turbaned dude that was balls-deep inside me suddenly grunted, his thrusts getting a little harder, then he let out a yell, slowing as he drove his cum deep into my guts. Once he was done, he rested his forehead on my back, panting, and I thanked him for his contribution, then asked him if he could make sure the door was latched on his way out.

Now that I was alone, I could finally give myself a well-earned orgasm. I started by gently teasing the stretched-out rim of my hole with my fingers, slowly dipping them into my wrecked ass to swirl the thick cocktail of slippery cum inside me. I groaned, humping the pillow as my dick got harder, wishing my ass was loose enough to shove my whole fist inside it. I had four fingers knuckles deep in my gash when I heard the door creak open.

"Dammit." My orgasm would have to wait. I pulled my hand out of my ass and adjusted my position—I didn't even look at the guy, just buried my face in the pillow and spread my thighs, readying myself to take another load. How could I possibly refuse? I was a cumslut through and through.

The new guy took his sweet time, squeezing my ass cheeks in a way that felt nice before pushing the fat head of his cock against my dripping hole.

Holy *shit*. Dude was *huge*.

I gasped, grabbing at the duvet to brace myself as his monster cock split me in two.

"Oh wow," I said, panting, and I heard him chuckle.

"Sorry." He obviously *wasn't* sorry because he started fucking me so hard and deep that I was having difficulty catching my breath between moans of pain and pleasure. But there was *something* . . . something about his voice that reminded me of . . . someone.

"Oh, *Jesus*, that's good," he said, slamming his dick deep and churning the mingled cum of strangers into a slurry that ran down my crack and soaked my jock-covered ballsack. "Oh fuck. Oh *fuck*, your wrecked cunt feels good on my fat cock. That's it, Sport . . . spread those fucking cheeks."

My eyes popped open, suddenly placing the voice. *Sport? Oh shit oh shit oh shit.* I peeked to my left, where he'd rested his hand when he'd gone up on one knee to properly impale me with his dick. I desperately hoped I was wrong, but my fears were confirmed when I saw the familiar black-and-chrome watch with a red dial on his wrist. I couldn't help but turn my head to see his face . . . and, in doing so, showed him mine.

He gasped, his face red and eyes wide, and I realized he was cumming hard, but now filled with the knowledge that it was his nephew's ass he was breeding and not some rando in a cheap hotel room.

He pulled out, his mouth working like he was trying to get words together but couldn't, and fell backwards to the carpet.

I turned over and sat up in the growing puddle of cum, horrified, my heart pounding and my mouth dry as I watched Uncle Zach get to his feet, his hands shaking as he did up his zipper.

Without a word, he left.

"Shit." My favourite uncle just *fucked* me. How the fuck does that even happen?

I grabbed my phone and set my screen name back to "cumslut2004", then ran to the door to lock it before anyone else came in. My back against the door, I brought up my profile on the app, wondering why Uncle Zach hadn't recognized me and only then remembered I had swapped out pics of my face for pics of my ass the week before.

Shit shit shit shit shit. What was I going to do?

My uncle's cum is inside me. I panted, closing my eyes. Jesus . . . it was all sorts of fucked up, but at the same time . . . *Oof.* I pinched my nipple as I let out a little moan. *My uncle just fucked me with his massive cock and came inside me. Uncle Zach just fucked me. Fucked me hard. Uncle Zach fucked my cummy hole with his monster dick and bred me deep.*

I kept it up, repeating variations of it like a mantra while I got harder and harder, and I scooped cum out of my ass to slather my cock with, wishing *all* of it was my uncle's as I quickly jerked off.

"Your uncle just used you like a fleshlight," I said out loud, stroking my cock. "Uncle Zach stretched out your sloppy ass and filled you with his cum. You fucked your uncle."

I grunted, breathing hard through clenched teeth as I emptied my balls, rivulets of cum leaking out of my ass and down my inner thighs with every pulse, my heart crashing against my ribcage and knees so weak I nearly collapsed with the last spasm of orgasm.

Drained, I staggered to the bed and fell face-first on the duvet.

Uncle Zach *fucked* me. *Jesus.* Now what? How is one supposed to react to that sort of thing? Probably not the way I had, obviously, but what would happen now? Were we supposed to pretend it didn't happen?

Was he going to avoid me? Was he going to tell someone? I pinched the bridge of my nose. And what about my dad's birthday party next week? Surely Zach wouldn't miss that.

I grinned. Handsome Uncle Zach and his huge cock . . .

TWO
WAS IT REALLY A MISTAKE?

"Put the cups on the table, Owen. Not on the sideboard." Mom pointed to the already heavily laden table, her other hand whisking away at the frosting she'd forgotten to make the night before.

"Sorry," I said, finding room for the stack of cups. Most of the guests had already arrived and were mingling in my parents' large sitting room. Some were family, others were my parents' friends, including some of Dad's work buddies. But one guest was conspicuously absent: my dad's youngest brother.

"Did Zach say he was going to make it?" I asked casually as I took the saran wrap off the potato salad.

"That's the second time you've asked," Mom replied, tasting the icing. "He said he was coming, but you know your uncle . . ." My mother rolled her eyes. She liked her brother-in-law but found him a little flaky.

"Hm." I was trying not to get my hopes up. I was starting to think he wasn't going to show.

As I arranged crackers and brie on a serving platter, I heard the front door open and Uncle Zach yell, "So, where's the birthday boy?"

While family members and friends jostled to crowd around my uncle, I slipped off to the side to watch him. Everyone *loved* Uncle

Zach, even our homophobic neighbour who just thought he "hadn't met the right girl yet." I leaned against the wall as he kiss-kissed his way through my cousins and aunts and then smirked when my mom came around the corner to pinch his cheek as he handed her a bottle of wine.

My uncle really was handsome. He looked a lot like my dad—blond hair, dark eyes, a Roman nose, and the same athletic build—but there was something extra special about him. From his tousled "just out of bed" hair to the way his sleeves were rolled halfway up his tanned forearms . . . he was just so damn sexy. I'd always had a little crush on my favourite uncle—he was only eleven years older than me and was just *so* cool—but now, because of what had happened in the hotel, that crush had teeth, and it was *hungry*.

Uncle Zach spotted me against the wall, and he froze for a split second, his expression unreadable. Then he broke into a smile, walked up to me and said, "Hey, Sport!" and ruffled my hair like he always did. Like nothing had happened. Like he hadn't put his dick into me.

"Hey, Uncle Zach." I tried sounding as laid back as possible despite my cheeks getting hot. Then he was off to socialize with his sister and brothers, and I was forgotten.

I didn't know how to feel. Was I disappointed? *Yes.* But wasn't that to be expected? Going forward, were we supposed to pretend that nothing had happened?

I finished my glass of wine and refilled it, watching my uncle charm everyone.

"You okay, honey?" My mom looked up at me with a comma of worry between her brows.

"Yeah. I'm fine." I forced myself to smile. "I was just thinking about something."

"Okay." She smiled and pushed her dark curls out of her eyes, depositing a streak of icing on her cheek in the process. "Why don't you come help me put out the rest of the dishes and cutlery?"

"Sure, Mom," I said, eyes darting to Uncle Zach. "I'll be there in a sec."

. . .

THERE WERE NEVER enough chairs to do a proper sit-down supper whenever my parents hosted. Everyone just took a plate, loaded it up and headed to the sitting room, either finding a spot on one of the couches or ottoman or eating standing up. Uncle Zach kept moving from group to group . . . and I was his shadow. I was at his elbow when he was talking to my dad's work friends. When he went to refill his plate and compliment my mom on her cooking, I followed and stood across from him, forcing him to look me in the eye as he talked. I chased him to the sitting room, where I perched next to him on the couch while he talked to his sister, our thighs touching because of lack of space. Then he excused himself, and I watched him cross through the sunroom to the bathroom beyond, waited a few seconds, then excused myself too. When he emerged from the bathroom and saw me there lying in wait, he let out a frustrated sigh.

"What do you want, Owen?" he asked in a harsh whisper as he came closer. We were the same height, so we saw eye to eye, and I couldn't help but notice how kissable his lips were.

"I want to talk," I whispered back. My heart pounded, and I clenched my fists to steady myself. "About what happened the other night."

"*Nothing* happened," he replied . . . but there was this, I don't know . . . this *look* in his eyes.

"I haven't been able to get it out of my head. It's all I think about." I let out a shaky breath. "Do you think about it too?"

At that moment, one of my mom's friends entered the sunroom, surprising us. Uncle Zach froze in place, so I grabbed him by the arm, unwilling to let the interruption get in the way of our conversation, and dragged him to the basement steps. He pulled his arm out of my grasp but followed me down the stairs, his mouth set in a hard line. I ducked into the big walk-in pantry and leaned back against the big chest freezer on the far wall, crossing my arms.

"So. *Do* you think about it?" I asked, feeling bolder now that we were alone. I smiled when I saw the flush creep up his neck. "Do you think about what happened?"

He rubbed his face with both hands before answering.

"Owen. It was a mistake."

"Mistake or not . . . have you been thinking about me? Come on. It's an easy question. Yes or no?" I said, cocking my head. "Have you been thinking about how—" I took a deep breath, going for broke "—how you slid your big, *thick* cock into me?"

"Owen." He licked his lips. I knew I had him when I saw how hard he was breathing, so I took a step forward.

"I think about it all the time. I think about how you *slammed* your massive dick into my ass. I think about how you pounded my hole, nice and deep. I think about how you bred my wet boy cunt with your huge load of hot cum."

My uncle stood there looking like a deer in headlights, a thin sheen of sweat on his upper lip.

"Jesus Christ, Owen."

"Yeah. You think about it, don't you?" I said, getting a little closer. I thought for a second that he would retreat a step, but he just closed his eyes and swallowed, his Adam's apple slowly bobbing. *"Don't you?"*

A few seconds ticked by, then Uncle Zach gave a shallow nod.

"Do you want to fuck me again?"

His eyes popped open, and his forehead wrinkled up.

"You don't even have to say anything—I *know* you do." I reached out and gently cupped the big bulge in the front of his jeans. His dick was already hard, but I felt it stiffen further as I squeezed it. *"See?* You want me. And I want you too."

Uncle Zach's nostrils flared as I toyed with his cock through his jeans, his eyes getting unfocused.

"Please?" I whispered. *"Please* fuck me."

"When?" he asked in a quiet, hoarse voice.

"Right now."

He swallowed again, and the muscles bulged under the dark blond stubble as he clenched his jaw. Then his expression changed.

The uncertainty was gone, replaced by a lusty, heavy-lidded glare. He turned and quietly closed the door, then pushed me back against the chest freezer. My heart felt like it was going to explode, it was beating so hard, and my legs had gone weak. *Oh my god, yes.* He went to turn me around, presumably to bend me over the freezer, but I stopped him.

"No," I said, literally panting with excitement, "I want to see your face while you fuck me." I slipped my shorts down with numb hands.

"Fine." He sounded almost angry, which just turned me on even more.

I scooted up onto the freezer, the top cold against my ass, and I opened my thighs, grabbing at my uncle's belt to tug him towards me. I had his belt, button, and zipper undone in a few seconds, and he pushed his hips into me to press his boxer-trapped boner into my shaved balls. I saw him peer around, hunting for something, and I guessed he was looking for something to use as lube.

"Don't worry—I lubed up before you arrived," I said, wrapping my legs around his waist.

"Huh . . . You were *that* sure I'd agree, eh?" he asked, shaking his head. He rasped out a quiet laugh. "Jesus."

He took a step back, dropped his pants, and out sprang his cock. It looked even bigger than I remembered, as big as a baby's arm. I grinned, spreading my ass cheeks wide to show him my hole.

"Fuck me, Uncle Zach."

That's all it took. He grabbed my legs and threw them over his shoulders before pushing his cock against my pucker. I whimpered as he breached me, his thick dick cleaving a path inside me, and I gasped at the sudden pain, my hands flying up to his chest to try to slow him, but he just chuckled and drove himself in deep.

"You said you wanted it, so shut up and take it, you little slut."

I don't think I'd ever been so turned on in my entire life. I let out a soft moan, the pain already gone and forgotten, his cock filling me up, stretching me open—it was like being fucked by a baseball bat, and it felt incredible.

"Oh *fuck*." He thrust into me hard a few times. "Christ, your ass wasn't this tight the other night."

"Yeah, well, you're the first one in this time." I grimaced as my head began to hit the wall from the force of his fucking. "Ow."

He curled his arms around my thighs and, without pulling his cock out, dragged me across the freezer top until I was lying down, then grabbed under my knees to take my legs off his shoulders, supporting and holding them wide open while he resumed rough-ploughing my ass.

I panted, my hands clutching the freezer top to either side of my hips to keep me from sliding, and closed my eyes, focusing on the big cock wrecking my hole. Something was happening to me that had only happened a few times in my life—my dick was getting hard from being fucked . . . and not half-assed hard either. Was it because of Uncle Zach's size, or was it because I was getting off on fucking a blood relative? Maybe both. I moaned again, wanting to grab my dick to jerk off but not daring to let go of the freezer.

When I started whimpering in time to Uncle Zach's thrusts, he leaned down over me, bending me over double . . . and *kissed* me. I think he'd only intended to shut me up because I was starting to make a lot of noise, but the second his lips met mine, I felt this crazy electricity crackle through me, making me give up my desperate hold on the freezer to wrap my arms around his shoulders, tonguing his mouth deep. The kiss felt frantic and keenly passionate in a way I'd never experienced before, and from the way his thrusts slowed as he concentrated on my mouth, I knew he felt it too.

Pulling away, Uncle Zach stared down at me, panting. I'm pretty sure my face mirrored the dazed look I saw in his.

"Wow," I whispered.

He huffed out two quick breaths and captured my mouth again with his, our tongues exploring the incredible, sizzling energy between us as his cock once again moved inside me, fucking me harder, his thrusts gathering speed.

I broke the kiss, pushing my pelvis up to drive him deeper.

"Your dick feels so good, Uncle Zach," I rasped. "Oh *god*, I'm gonna cum."

However, my uncle's head jerked up right then, and he froze, his eyes wide, and I heard it too—someone was coming down the basement stairs.

"Shit." He pulled his dick out of me, yanking up his pants as we stared at each other in a panic. I sat up and led him quickly into the adjacent room, closing the door behind us as silently as I could. It was a tiny closet-sized room my family had dubbed the "furnace room" even though it only held the hot water tank and a shelf stacked with storage bins—I couldn't think of a reason why anyone would want to go in there, so I figured we were probably safe.

Uncle Zach and I pressed our ears to the unpainted drywall, listening as someone entered the big pantry room. It was only when the freezer door opened with a loud creak that I remembered leaving my shorts on the floor. *Shit*. I hoped they would go unnoticed.

"I don't see it," Aunt Alice called out, and I heard my mother's muffled reply from upstairs. "It's *where*?" my aunt shouted. I could hear her rummaging in the chest freezer.

Uncle Zach surprised me right then. He pulled my hips back against him and slid his cock up into me, my tender asshole throbbing as it swallowed his shaft to the balls, and I couldn't help the gasp that burst out of me.

Aunt Alice went silent, and Zach stilled for a moment, listening. Then, when she resumed her search for whatever my mother had asked for, he wrapped one hand around my re-hardening dick and covered my mouth with the other, fucking me slowly. As soon as Aunt Alice tromped back up the basement steps, Zach started fucking me faster, his lips near my ear.

"How's that slutty hole feel now, Sport? Does it love your uncle's cock?" His breath was warm on my neck, his voice low and husky. "I think it does, doesn't it?"

I could only nod and moan closed-lipped against Uncle Zach's palm. He stroked my dick faster, my precum making his hand slippery as he worked it over my cockhead, and I closed my eyes tight as he began driving himself so deep that he nearly lifted me off the floor with each upward thrust.

"I'm gonna put a big load inside this sloppy little cunt of yours," he murmured almost gently, but I could hear the strain in his voice as he got closer to climax. "And then we're going to go back upstairs to the party, and every *single* time I smile at you, you're going to think to yourself, 'I'm Uncle Zach's personal fuckhole,' and you're going to keep those cheeks squeezed tight, so you don't lose a *drop* of my cum, and then after the party I'm gonna take you back to my place and put another load into you."

Even before he'd finished speaking the last word, I let out a strained cry and actually heard my cum hit the wall.

Uncle Zach laughed quietly, jerking my dick as I came, each pulse rippling my swollen hole around the stiff shaft buried inside me—the more my asshole tried to clamp shut while being held wide open by his thick cock, the harder I came. By the end, my knees were like jelly, so my uncle had to push me hard against the wall to hold me up, fucking me faster and faster before he suddenly stilled. Then, letting out a deep growl that vibrated against my back, I felt his dick throb inside me, breeding me deep.

I couldn't have been happier.

We stayed put like that, just catching our breaths, and when he finally pulled out, I staggered a bit, losing my footing—as if the only thing keeping me standing had been his dick.

"You okay there, Sport?" he asked, zipping up his jeans. He was flushed and bright-eyed, his hair even more tousled than usual.

"Mmhmm." I gave him a dazed grin. I couldn't remember when I'd let someone other than me jerk my dick.

He shook his head slowly, his eyes on mine. "*Christ*. This is *so* fucked up." Uncle Zach exhaled hard. "But—" he cupped my face, pulling me in to kiss my lips a few times "—I just want to kiss you and kiss you and *Jesus* . . ." He looked down. "Just give me ten minutes, and I'll be hard enough to fuck you all over again."

I grinned wider, then sobered. "Hey, uh, did you mean what you said?"

"When?" he asked, looking confused.

"When you were fucking me?"

"Oh." Uncle Zach's face flushed, and he ducked his head, rubbing at his nape. "Um, my mouth just sorta runs on autopilot. It's got a mind of its own."

"Oh," I replied, disappointed.

He frowned at my expression. "But . . . what part?"

"About you taking me back to your place."

Uncle Zach smiled. "You wanna come back to my place after the party?"

"*Fuck* yes."

"Good." His eyes darkened. "I'll take you home and hold you down and give you a good, thorough fucking and gape that slutty hole of yours." He let out a low growl and pinned me against the wall, tonguing my mouth open to kiss me, but he pulled away too soon, breathing hard. "I guess I don't even need ten minutes." He laughed, looking down at the prominent bulge in his jeans.

I reached for him, but he stepped back.

"Owen, we have to get back to the party," he said, adjusting his dick. "People are going to wonder where we are—we've been gone a while."

I sighed. "Yeah. You're right."

He reached out and gently grabbed the back of my neck. "But, we'll leave early. Promise."

"We *can't* leave before the birthday cake."

Uncle Zach squeezed my neck, grinning. "Okay . . . how about we leave right after?"

"Okay. Yeah. Uh . . . you go up first," I said. "I'll meet you up there—I gotta clean that up." I looked over at the splash of cum on the wall. There was a long streak of it, dripping into a puddle on the bare concrete floor.

"And . . . put some pants on," he said, releasing me.

I laughed, glancing down. "*Right.*"

. . .

WHEN I GOT BACK UPSTAIRS, Uncle Zach was deep in a conversation with my father and aunt, but there was nowhere to sit, so I hovered nearby, wishing I could speed time up so we could leave. I clenched my ass, thinking about the load Uncle Zach had fucked into me, and I let out a shaky breath, quickly fixing my boner so that it was wedged between my belly and the waistband of my shorts. I glanced around, hoping no one was watching me and was startled to see my mother had silently materialized next to me.

"*There* you are," she said. "I've been looking all over for you. Do you know where the birthday candles are?"

"Um. No?"

She frowned up at me. "Are you feeling okay? You're all flushed." Mom put the back of her hand against my forehead.

"I'm fine," I said. Unable to resist, I glanced over at my uncle. He was smiling at his sister, but I had the distinct impression that he had just been looking my way. Shit, at this rate, people were going to start wondering what the hell was going on with the two of us. I realized that the sooner the candles were found, the sooner the birthday cake would be served . . . and then off to Uncle Zach's to get good and ploughed. "They might be in the junk drawer. Here, I'll help you look."

THREE
UNCLE ZACH'S HOUSE

WE COULDN'T LEAVE RIGHT after the cake as we had planned—my mother insisted we take pictures first since we weren't all together that often, and then we had to wait until she printed out copies.

"I don't know what's going on with your face here," Mom said, handing me mine. "But, thankfully, everyone else looks nice."

I did have a bizarre expression in the group shot, a sort of wide-eyed, startled look, but that's because Uncle Zach had slipped his hand down the back of my shorts as my mother took the picture. I smiled, realizing I'd think of that every time I saw it.

"Thanks, Mom," I said, then furrowed my brow, eyes darting to my uncle. "You know . . . um, maybe I'm *not* feeling so great after all."

"Do you want to lie down upstairs?" Mom asked, looking worried.

"I don't know. I think maybe I should go home."

"Actually, I have to go too," Uncle Zach said, picking up on my cue. "Hey, why don't I give you a lift home, Owen? You're on the way."

"Oh! Only if you don't mind," I replied, my pulse racing as I played along. "I'd really appreciate it."

"Not a problem."

. . .

Twenty minutes later, after the endless goodbyes, Uncle Zach and I were finally on the road. Soon, I had one hand locked around the door grip while the other clutched the chest strap of my seatbelt so hard my fingers were cramping.

"Do you always drive like a maniac?" I shouted over the roaring wind as his little silver convertible zipped around a pickup truck that had the audacity to do the speed limit.

Uncle Zach glanced over at me, his white-toothed grin wide in his tanned face.

"Oh my god—*eyes on the road!*" I screamed, my heart in my throat.

He just laughed and turned up the music as he passed precariously close to a minivan. Old school heavy metal blasted from the speakers, competing with the wind, and he sang along with the unintelligible lyrics while I sat there rigid with terror. Finally, after looking over at me a few times, he realized my fear was authentic.

"Give me your hand," he shouted above the din, holding his hand out to me. Nervously, I released the seatbelt strap and reached out, thinking he wanted to hold hands to make me feel better, but instead, he placed my hand on his crotch. Under my palm, I felt his dick move.

"To take your mind off my driving," he yelled, shooting me another mischievous grin.

I licked my lips—my throat was so dry I could barely swallow. Having my hand on my uncle's dick certainly distracted me, but his car was so low to the ground that anyone in a pickup or SUV could look over and see where my hand was.

Uncle Zach said something else, but the wind and music drowned it out.

"*What?*" I yelled.

"I said, take my dick out!"

"People will see!" I shouted.

He shrugged. "Who cares?" He'd already taken care of the top button of his jeans, and I couldn't help but give in and help him with the zipper. Excitement was quickly taking over my fear. Jaw clenched, I took my eyes off the road and slid my fingers through the opening in his boxers, panting out a few breaths when I felt along his stiff shaft. It took a little effort and some wiggling adjustments on his part, but I soon had his boner free and began stroking it, trying not to think about how we were absolutely *screaming* down the highway. Part of me was super turned on, but another part wondered what people would say if we crashed and died and they found Uncle Zach with his dick out. A crazed giggle burst out of me, and I shook my head, squeezing my eyes shut tight so I could put all my concentration into the thick cock in my hand.

A FEW MINUTES LATER, the car swerved, and I thought: *Shit, this is it* in a panic before opening my eyes to find that we were not about to crash and die a horrible and possibly scandalous death—just taking an exit. Uncle Zach slowed as we took a few turns, ending up in a residential area, and he turned down the music as he smiled at me.

"See? Safe and sound," he said.

I nodded, my hand slowing on his dick as I stared at the houses to either side of us. It was a rich neighbourhood, the kind where people gave out full-sized chocolate bars at Halloween, but the further we went, the bigger the houses got and the more land there was between them. I frowned, wondering where we were, and Uncle Zach put his hand over mine to get it moving again.

"Yeah, keep going," he said, releasing my hand to work the stick shift as he sped up.

Watching his expression, I shifted my grip, harvesting a warm drop of precum from the slit to use as lube to stroke him with, and smiled when I saw his lips part and brow furrow. Eventually, I moved my hand so it cupped the head of his dick, his slippery precum letting me concentrate on his cockhead, swirling my palm over the top of it repeatedly until he was squirming in his seat.

"Stop! Stop… *stop…*" Uncle Zach grabbed my wrist. He looked over at me, a noticeable flush mottling his neck and cheeks. "*Fuck* that was close." He turned back to the road, gunning the engine again as he worked the shift stick. "Hang on!"

I looked around, only just noticing then that we were on a stretch of road bordered by trees, not a house in sight.

"Where the hell *are* we?" I asked.

Uncle Zach laughed. "Never been this far west, eh?" He suddenly leaned forward, peering through the windshield. "Ah! *There's* a good spot."

He wrenched the wheel, and the car turned right, bumping down onto a narrow, barely visible gravel road. I assumed we had arrived at his place, but he quickly jerked the wheel in the opposite direction, parking us parallel to the main road, and killed the engine. Uncle Zach then reached over and opened the glove compartment, fishing around for something. Finally, he got out, jogged to my side, his boner still protruding from his jeans, and pulled my door open.

"Get out."

Confused, I did as I was told, only to have him slam the door shut and turn me around, pushing me over the side of the car as he yanked down the back of my shorts.

"What are you—" I looked over and saw him squeezing something onto his cock. "What's that?"

"Just a little aloe vera gel. I got a sunburn a few weeks ago," he said, distracted by what he was doing.

"On your *dick?*"

He looked up, his eyebrows high, and snorted. "I didn't burn my dick, smart-ass. I'm just using it as lube."

Then, without another word, he shoved me hard against the car and leaned into me, his hand guiding his cock between my ass cheeks, searching for my pucker, and I gasped as his cock forced my hole open. I couldn't believe he was just going to do this in public— a large bush only partially hid us—but he started fucking me hard and fast, grunting into his thrusts, oblivious to the cars that kept passing us on the main road.

After only a dozen quick thrusts, he let out a groan, pushing himself balls-deep, and I felt his dick twitch and jerk as he came inside me. Then, with a breathy chuckle, he pulled out when he was done, leaving me hanging over the passenger door as he got back in the car. I stared at him, my heart pounding. *What have I gotten myself into?*

"C'mon . . . get in, Sport."

A little shaky, I straightened and awkwardly pulled my shorts up, staring at his profile as he keyed the engine. I opened the door and silently took my seat, buckling in.

Without looking at me, Uncle Zach said, "Sorry, I couldn't wait." He turned the convertible back onto the main road, grinning from ear to ear as he accelerated. Releasing the stick shift, he put his hand on my knee and glanced over. "Don't worry . . . I'm not done with you yet."

Swallowing thickly, I nodded, my cheeks hot. I felt . . . *used*. Vulnerable. Close to tears, even.

I was so happy.

Not even ten minutes later, Uncle Zach pulled off the main road onto a narrow private road hedged in by tall pines and birch trees. At the end of it, a big iron gate opened via the remote clipped to the driver's side sunshade, and once we were through, my uncle turned off the car stereo and smiled as we drove through the leafy tunnel in silence. Once we emerged, I blinked in surprise. Surrounded by dense forest was a large clearing, and at the centre was a futuristic building that resembled three stacked boxes made entirely of plate-glass, chrome, and wood siding stained so dark it was nearly black. I stared up at the structure as the convertible went around to park under a second-floor deck supported by two massive concrete pillars, creating an open-air garage.

Uncle Zach got out of the car, and I followed suit, staring off in a daze. The rear of the house looked over water—a lake or a river, I couldn't tell—and a large powerboat was moored at the end of a pier. I turned to my uncle, and he smiled at me as he pulled a charging cable out of a panel in the wall and plugged it into the socket in the convertible.

"Holy shit, this is where you live?" I asked.

"Oh, right!" he said, raking his wind-tousled hair back from his forehead. "You were on a camping trip when I had the fam over for brunch last summer. You never saw my new place."

"Yeah." He was *rich*? How had I missed that? I looked at the silver convertible with fresh eyes. I had been so distracted by my uncle taking me back to his place that I had failed to register that his car was something seriously high-end, maybe even custom—I hadn't known they even made electric cars with manual transmissions.

Uncle Zach tilted his head, his brow furrowing. "When was the last time you visited me?"

"You were living in that weird house near the university with those two guys."

"Jesus. That was like… eight years ago?"

"Ten." I remembered it vividly. It had been a birthday request to my parents—to pay a solo visit to my favourite uncle. He'd taken me out to see *The Hobbit: The Desolation of Smaug*, and then we had Mexican food afterwards, and when we got back to his place, he'd let me have a beer. It was one of my favourite memories.

"Ah. Then you completely missed the McMansion I made the mistake of buying when CAI took off."

"CAI?"

"CunningAI. We do custom algorithms. At this point, every big gaming company has something by us. And we have a few contracts with the Canadian government and lots of municipalities here in Quebec and in Ontario. Oh, and a whole bunch of post-production houses in Montreal, the States, and India. Plus, a few other companies use us to test shit out for them."

"Oh. Uh, Mom told me a while back that your 'little business' was 'doing okay,' " I replied, doing air quotes.

"I mean, shit . . . she's been to the house." He shook his head and grinned. "If this is 'doing okay,' I'd love to see what 'doing great' looks like to her."

"You know my mom . . . she doesn't like to make a big deal out of anything." I shrugged.

Uncle Zach laughed and then beckoned me with a jerk of his head to follow him around to the front of the house.

"So, what do you think?"

I looked up at the house, taking it all in again, then I grinned and met my uncle's gaze. "About the fact that you're handsome, sexy, *and* rich?"

"You like that, eh?" He narrowed his eyes. "I've got a feeling that there are a few other things about me you'll like . . ." I thought he was going to kiss me, but he just gave a low chuckle and turned away, pressing his thumb against a black square next to the front door. The lock clicked audibly, and he pushed the door open, gesturing for me to go in.

The interior was less "chromed-cube" than the exterior and was decorated with accents that mirrored the woods outside the vast floor-to-ceiling windows in the living room to my left. A set of comfy-looking red couches sat across from each other, a fashionable resin and wood coffee table in between them, and the fireplace against the far wall wouldn't have been out of place in a rich guy's hunting lodge. No taxidermy though, thank god.

In front of me and to my right was a huge kitchen with a long centre island and four stools. The appliances were all shiny and stainless steel, and the countertops were butcher's block. It took me a second to realize the whole backsplash beneath the upper cupboards was a window that looked out over the lake.

"Wow, this place is uh… *wow*. Seriously."

"*I* think so," Uncle Zach said, watching me look around.

"And what's up there?" I asked, pointing to the stairs with my chin.

"What do *you* think?"

I felt my face get a little warm. My ass was still tender from the beating it had taken, but I doubted he'd be able to get hard enough to fuck me again so soon. It had been what, fifteen minutes since he bent me over on the side of the road? We could still fool around, though. "I'd like to go see."

Uncle Zach's smile stretched slowly as he stepped toward me, but then he stopped and frowned. "Wait, hang on a sec." He walked back to the front door and pressed a button on a small panel. "Lior? You home?" He released the button and listened for a response from the small speaker below it.

Lior? I clenched my jaw, my guts twisting. "Who's Lior? Your boyfriend?" I asked, trying to keep my voice light and free of the cocktail of apprehension, jealousy, and disappointment that had started simmering in my belly.

Obviously, I did a lousy job of hiding my feelings because Uncle Zach chuckled, his gaze fondly teasing. "And what if he *was*?" He kept his eyes on mine while I internally squirmed, trying to come up with an answer that didn't sound stupid or needy. Then he laughed again and put his hands around my waist, pulling me closer. "Don't worry. He's not my boyfriend, Sport."

I swallowed and nodded, breathing out as he cupped my backside with both hands.

"What is he, then?" I said, only managing a hoarse whisper because right then, he squeezed my ass cheeks and pushed his denim-clad boner against mine. It looked like I *would* get another load, as he promised.

"Uh, well, Lior cleans up after me. Does the groceries, cooks a few nights a week . . . that sort of thing. Makes sure I pay my bills on time."

"So, like a servant. A manservant?" I laughed. "Or a . . . butler?"

"I guess he's something like that," Uncle Zach replied, ducking his head to kiss up the side of my neck. He kept talking in a murmur, his lips sliding over my skin, making me shiver. "He goes to temple with his mom on Saturdays and *usually* spends the night there because it's a two-hour drive, so we have the place to ourselves."

I felt my breath hitch as his teeth closed gently on my earlobe. I licked my lips, a question gnawing at my insides.

"Uncle Zach?"

"Mm?"

"Have you two ever fucked?" I whispered. He stopped nibbling at my neck and pulled back, and I instantly regretted my question.

"Yes," he replied, his brow furrowed. "On occasion, Lior and I fuck."

"Okay," I said quietly.

"Why? Does that bother you?" He peered into my eyes, studying my expression.

"No," I lied.

Uncle Zach pinched my chin softly between thumb and forefinger and brought my mouth to his for a chaste little kiss, and then he drew back. "Oh, my jealous little nephew." He clucked his tongue, shaking his head.

Wondering if I screwed up, I sighed, my chest tight.

"I'm sorry."

"*Relax*, Sport. It's casual, me and Lior," he said, resting his forearms on my shoulders. He pushed his pelvis against mine, nudging my boner again with his. "I think you'll get it when you meet him."

"Okay," I replied, knowing I didn't sound convinced. Whoever this Lior was, I *really* didn't want to meet him now.

Narrowing his eyes at me again, my uncle grinned a little crookedly, a deep dimple appearing in one cheek. "I kinda like that you're jealous, Sport. It's cute."

"Yay." I glared at him.

Uncle Zach leaned in again for a kiss, coaxing my mouth open so he could tongue me deep, taking my breath away and driving every thought out of my head.

His eyes were dark with lust when he released me, and he breathed hard as he grabbed my hand.

"C'mon . . . let's go upstairs."

I just nodded and followed him eagerly up the wide staircase.

His bedroom took up the whole second floor. On the far side of the room was another huge floor-to-ceiling window with a home gym and a treadmill in front of it. To my right was a double set of patio doors beneath a line of four round windows that looked like ship's portals, and beyond the doors was the big deck we had parked under. To my left were a series of flat black doors—a wardrobe, I assumed—with chrome handles shaped like those silver things on boats you tie ropes to. I'd have to ask him what those were called. The few visible pieces of wall were painted a dark navy, and the floor was wood, stained grey-black and installed on the diagonal. The king-sized pedestal bed was right in the centre of the room, the bedding crisp and white.

"Wow. Tidy," I said, thinking about the clothes on my bedroom floor.

"Yup. That's what I pay Lior for," Uncle Zach replied.

When you're not fucking him. I pushed the thought out of my head and turned straight into my uncle's arms. He kissed me hard, forcing my head back as he took command of my mouth with his tongue, his hands clawing at my ass. Pushing against me, he made me take a backwards step and then another, guiding me toward the bed. When he pulled up on my t-shirt, I broke the kiss so he could pull it over my head.

Grinning, he tweaked one of my nipples hard, making me gasp at the sudden pain.

"D'you have a safe word, Sport?" he asked, running his hand up softly from my belly to the centre of my chest.

"Huh? Um . . ." I licked my lips, distracted by his touches. "Yeah, it's 'pineapple.' "

"Pineapple? Gotcha." And with that, he suddenly shoved me hard, and I fell back, landing with a thump on the bed.

"Hey!" I said, my heart beating fast. I hadn't realized how close we were to the bed.

"Hey, yourself," he said, laughing. "Scoot back and ditch the shorts."

Doing as I was told, I crawled backwards on the mattress to make room for him and threw my shorts off the side, then watched as he unbuttoned his shirt. Uncle Zach had dressed preppy since I could remember—jeans or khaki pants with a dress shirt or a nice henley—but as his buttons came undone and his shirt parted, I could only gape in surprise, realizing I'd only seen him naked from the waist down so far.

His chest was *covered* in tattoos. I could make out roses, skulls, birds, some spikey lettering, and a compass, and as he pulled the shirt completely off, he revealed his arms were also inked nearly to the elbow. I was so amazed by the tattoos that I didn't register he had both nipples pierced until he tilted his head, grinning as he toyed with the bar through the left one.

"Holy shit," I said, my voice hoarse.

"Told you there were other things you'd like about me." Then he ducked his head, his eyes still on mine, and gave me a slow grin as he leaned down to drop his jeans. "Oh, I'm going to enjoy tearing that cunt of yours apart again." He stood, his thick cock jutting out in a stiff arc, the slit already glistening with precum—I swallowed, honestly a little nervous about the predatory gleam in his eyes, and watched as he went and opened one of the wardrobe doors to retrieve a bottle of lube from one of the drawers inside.

He slicked up his dick as he walked back to the bed, then climbed onto the mattress, grabbing me by the ankles to open my legs. Uncle Zach crawled between my thighs, and I was expecting him to kiss me or fondle me a little, but instead, he leaned over me and immediately jammed his cock into my sore hole without warning. I cried out, my whole body jerking as he grunted and forced his dick into me straight to the balls.

"Ow, *fuck*," I said, panting as my tears rose.

"Nah, you like it," he said, beginning to thrust into me despite my whimpers of pain.

He was absolutely right, though.

Crying out again as he fucked me ruthlessly, I "tried" to push him off me, but that only got my arms pinned above my head, his hands tight around my wrists as his cock pummeled my guts, his entire weight resting on me.

"Stop squirming, you slut," he said, his mouth near my ear, "or else I'll take my time with you. You think *this* hurts?" He laughed. "This is nothing."

I let out a shaky breath, my dick getting hard as he continued to fuck me, and I let out a pained gasp as he bit into the side of my neck.

"I'm going to breed you like the dirty little bitch that you are," he said, putting a growl in his voice. "And then you're gonna lick the cum off my cock, and you're gonna *thank* me... Do you know *why* you're gonna do that?"

I closed my eyes, wishing I could reach my needy boner, but even if I *could* get one hand free, my dick was trapped between us.

"B-because I'm a dirty little bitch?" I whispered.

"And what are you going to say?"

"Thank you?" I winced as he suddenly started fucking me faster. I groaned, my pain very real.

"That's a good slut . . . now shhh," he murmured. "It'll be over soon."

Panting, I lay there helplessly as he continued to "rape" me, my stretched-out hole getting raw as he kept at me for a dozen more thrusts. Letting out a loud grunt, he suddenly went still, and I gasped, feeling his dick swell and throb as he emptied his balls into me, breeding me good and deep for the third time that day.

Uncle Zach stayed on top of me long enough that I felt his cock start to slip out as it softened. After releasing my wrists, he went up on his elbows and looked down at me with a pleased grin, his cheeks pink from exertion and his eyes half-lidded. Without a word, he kissed me on the forehead before gently pulling out and leaving me alone on the bed. I watched him open the last of the black doors and enter the room beyond. I could see white tiles from my angle, so I assumed it was the bathroom.

I looked down at myself. My stomach and cock were drenched in precum, and my boner bobbed up of its own accord now that it was free. *What's going to happen now*? I was in pain, and both turned on and confused, which made me uncomfortable, but I didn't know if I was "allowed" to touch myself or even move. I squeezed my legs together, trying to ignore my burning hole.

Uncle Zach emerged from the bathroom with a small jar and a glass of water. I saw he'd cleaned his dick, which only confused me more.

"I thought I was supposed to take care of the cum on your cock," I said, getting up on my elbows.

He laughed. "I told you . . . my mouth has a mind of its own. Sometimes it's just dirty talk." Frowning, he sat on the bed beside me. "I'm sorry. Were you looking forward to it?"

"Actually . . . not really," I confessed. "Not sure how clean everything is after a day."

"Gotcha." He smiled, then held out the glass of water. "Here."

"Oh. Thanks." I accepted the glass and gulped it down in three swallows, only realizing then how thirsty I was.

Taking the empty glass from me, Uncle Zach had me lie back down and spread my legs again. Very gently, he used his fingers to smear the cool contents of the jar onto my throbbing pucker, working a little inside me as well. Almost immediately, my ass started feeling better, and I sighed in relief.

"That feel okay?" He asked, pulling his fingers out of me.

"Oh yeah. Wow. Thanks." The fact that he was taking care of me like this made my chest tight, so I cleared my throat, not wanting to seem clingy and immature, and asked, "Um, what is it?"

"There's a lady at the farmer's market that makes all kinds of balms. This one's a special batch she makes for me."

"Bust a lot of holes, eh?" I said, trying to keep the jealousy out of my voice. "Did you tell her that's what you needed it for?"

Uncle Zach laughed. I loved the way the late afternoon sun coming through the enormous windows made his hair reddish and brought out flecks of gold in his dark eyes.

"Basically. She's cool."

I smiled at him, then lifted my head to meet his kiss when he bent over me. This time, the kiss was tender and slow, and I let myself sink back onto the mattress as he began softly running his fingertips over my chest and nipples. Gradually, his hand made its way to my belly, and I felt him chuckle into our kiss as his fingers found the puddle of precum.

"Now it's time to take care of this, hm?" He said against my lips as he took my stiff dick in hand.

Moaning, I nodded, pushing up into his grasp as he began slowly jerking me off. However, he stopped after only a few strokes, causing me to groan in frustration.

"Patience, Sport. I've got something I think you'll like."

He got up from the bed, returning to the wardrobe drawers where he had found the lube, and took something out of a wooden box. Rejoining me on the bed, he showed me the toy. It was slim and black with a ribbed head that bulged forward, and the base was flat and narrow.

"If that's going in my ass . . . Uncle Zach, I'm too sore. Even with your special hole cream."

"Wuss," he said, kissing the tip of my nose. "I'm not going to fuck you with it. I'm just going to slide it into you, and it's going to sit against your P-spot and"—he pressed a hidden button on the base, and the toy began to hum, its lopsided head moving up and down and side to side—"make you feel good on the inside while I take care of your dick."

I frowned at the toy, curious but also apprehensive, considering the state of my ass. I'd never been one for toys, but if I was being honest, it's only because I was flat-broke most of the time and couldn't afford any.

"It's *tiny* compared to my dick, Sport. And I promise it'll blow your mind. What do you say?"

Swallowing, I relented and lay back again, parting my knees to give him access to my ass. The toy slid in without any pain, and I couldn't really feel it once it was in place. Then he turned it on.

"Woah," I said, closing my eyes. It was vibrating and moving, the ribbed head swirling over my prostate. "Holy shit."

"There are three speeds. Want me to make it go faster?"

"Uh." I squirmed a little. "No. No, this is fine."

He had me put my legs down, knees together on the bed, and with some lube in hand, began to jerk me off again.

"Do you like it?" he asked in a low voice.

"Dude, I'm gonna cum in like . . . no time," I said hoarsely, my ballsack already tightening.

"Do you want me to stop? Want me to draw it out? Make you beg for it?"

I laughed, then moaned as his hand tightened, his thumb swiping over my sensitive cockhole.

"Normally . . . n-normally, I'd say yes. But. Oh *god*." I whimpered as his hand left me. "No. No, *please* keep going. I promise you can torture the hell out of me next time, but I will cry if you stop now. *Literally*." The toy in my ass *did* feel great, but what I really wanted was my uncle's hand on my dick.

With a chuckle, Uncle Zach resumed jerking my cock with both hands, one following the other, so it felt like one continuous stroke, and I pretty much yelled when the first pulse of orgasm hit. My dick twitched hard in Uncle Zach's hand as my cum blasted out of it, and I'm sure if I hadn't had my legs together, the toy in my ass would have shot across the room with the force of my climax. As it was, it was pushed out while I quivered and moaned through the longest, most intense orgasm I'd ever had, and by the end of it, I *was* in tears.

Panting, I cracked one eye open when I finally regained control of my body and found my uncle staring at me with this dazed look on his face.

"What's wrong?" I croaked, my breath still hitching in my throat.

"You're fucking gorgeous when you cum," Uncle Zach said, his voice quiet.

I felt my cheeks burn.

I'm not good with compliments, so my first instinct was to dismiss or diminish his words. However, it felt . . . different being with him. I took a deep breath.

"Thank you."

Uncle Zach leaned down for another kiss, just a light brush of my parted lips.

"No. Thank *you*."

FOUR
STAY THE NIGHT?

EVIDENTLY, I passed out for a bit because I found myself alone in his bed sometime later. Outside the huge windows, the sun was starting to dip low over the lake. Rubbing my face, I sat up, wondering where my uncle had gone. I saw another of those little intercom boxes set into the bed's headboard, so I thumbed the button.

"Uncle Zach?" I let go and listened, but there was no answer. Then I saw movement on the deck outside the patio doors and grabbed my shorts to investigate. Uncle Zach was lying naked on a red lounge chair, reading something off a tablet. Shielding his eyes, he looked up at me as I approached.

"Hey, Sport." He smiled and then noticed my shorts. "You don't need those—it's not like I have neighbours. Take 'em off." Grinning wider, he reached up to tug on the leg of my shorts. "No clothes for you, kiddo. I want to see your dick and ass at all times. My house, my rules."

I laughed, feeling a bit embarrassed as I kicked off my shorts and stood there with my arms crossed.

"That's better," he said, returning to his tablet.

"Um. So . . . I don't want to overstay . . ." I said awkwardly. I looked around, noticing the covered hot tub at the far end of the large patio. *Nice.* I wondered if I'd get to try it out while I was here —I'd never been in one.

Uncle Zach glanced back up. "You have plans?"

"No."

"Well, then . . . how long you stay is up to you. I figured you were going to stay the night."

"Really?"

My uncle laughed. "Yes, really."

I nodded. "Okay. Thanks." I stared down at my feet. I was becoming uncomfortably aware of how much I needed a cleanse and a shower—between all the cum and sweat, I was starting to get a little ripe. "Can I take a shower?"

"Sure thing. There's an enema adapter in the shower if you want to use it. Or, if you prefer, there's a bulb kit in the cupboard under the sink. It's still in the box; no one's used it before. It's yours if you want it. You know where the lube is."

"Oh. Okay. Cool," I replied, relieved I didn't have to ask. "Thanks."

"You bet. And I just have to finish answering some emails, so if you're still in there when I'm done, I'll come join you."

THE SHOWER WAS a giant glass box with four different shower heads, including the enema wand adapter he had mentioned. I'd never used one before and was worried about getting the pressure and heat right, so I opted for the bulb. Usually, I liked to clean a little deeper and used a hanging enema bag, but my diet was specifically tailored for bottoming, so, honestly, the extra care I took was just me being over-cautious. I filled the bulb with warm water and got to work.

WHEN I FELT I was clean enough on the inside, I stepped into the shower and played around with the different settings until I had a combination rain shower from above and back massage from one of the smaller showerheads. I sighed happily, standing there in the warm water for a while, just enjoying it before soaping up with my uncle's fancy body wash. I was rinsing my hair when I heard the shower door click behind me. Turning, I smiled at Uncle Zach.

"I was wondering where you were," I said. I shut off the smaller showerhead and pulled him under the big square one overhead.

He wrapped his arms around me, wet skin sliding over wet skin as simulated rainfall trickled down over us, his mouth greedy as he kissed me, his hands cupping my ass. Eventually, he drew back, his teeth worrying his bottom lip as he shook his head at me.

"What is it about you?" he asked quietly, moving his hips from side to side, rubbing his hard dick against mine. "Jesus, you're like a drug, I swear."

I laughed, feeling self-conscious under his intense gaze.

"Turn around," he said, cocking his head with a grin. "Spread those cheeks for me. I want in."

"Again?" I asked, surprised. He was insatiable.

"*Yes*, again," he replied and, without waiting for me to move, grabbed my arm to spin me in place, roughly pushing me up against the glass. I heard a snap of a lid closing as he held me in place with one hand, then his big dick was punching at my hole all over again, forcing itself into my guts as I wailed and scrabbled against the slippery glass.

"Stop complaining. I *own* this pussy," he growled, his mouth by my ear. "It's *my* fuckhole, and if I feel like breeding it, that's what I'm going to do."

"Ow," I yelped. "Not so hard." I said it while pushing back against him, driving him deeper and harder on purpose.

"Did you hear me? Who owns your hole?"

I panted, my eyes closed. "You do."

"That's right. *My* hole."

"Ow. Yes." His thrusts began to slow, and I wondered if he was getting close.

"And I can use it for whatever the fuck I want." He stopped moving almost entirely, and I opened my eyes, confused, but then I felt pressure and heat in my guts and realized he was pissing into me. I gasped, trying to escape, but he wrapped one hand around my throat, holding me still as the pressure mounted inside me. Then he pulled out, and I felt his piss explode out of my ass, running in hot rivulets down the back of my legs as the flow tapered off, and I cried out as he immediately jammed his dick back into me to fill me up a second time, and a third. I was trembling and moaning, squirming as he used me for a toilet, equal parts shocked and excited. When his bladder was finally empty, he began fucking me once more, faster now, the last of the piss spurting out of my hole with every hard plunge until he yelled out, startling me as he sent yet another load of cum into my guts.

I felt dizzy and breathless, my legs trembling as he panted against my back, his cock softening slowly until it slipped out of my aching hole; then he turned me around to face him and held me tight as the warm water ran over our bodies. After I had calmed, he took a soft cloth and the bottle of body wash and gently scrubbed me all over, his touch so tender and attentive that I had tears in my eyes by the end of it.

Once I was clean once more, he quickly soaped up, rinsed, then turned off the water, wrapping me in a big fluffy towel after helping me out of the shower. Then he led me back to the big white bed, where he coaxed my dick to get hard again with kisses and gentle strokes.

"You're a good boy, Owen," he said, fondling my balls. "And a very good boy deserves to cum."

"Oh yeah?" I said drowsily, then hissed out my breath, arching my back off the bed as his tongue touched the head of my cock.

"Say it," he murmured, his lips teasing my shaft. "Say you're a good boy, and you deserve to cum."

"I'm a good boy, and I deserve to cum," I whispered, my eyes suddenly wet again. It felt so . . . *strange* to say the words but in a good way. I'd known for a long time that I liked being manhandled or used like an object. And I liked it when my partners were harsh or dominating . . . but this? This was new.

"Yes, you are." Uncle Zach's smile was warm, and his dark eyes tender as he stroked my dick, and my chest got so tight my breath started hitching like I was about to burst into sobs. "You're a very special boy, and I want to make you feel good. Now, tell me what you'd like—my mouth? My hands?" he asked. When I stayed silent, his brow wrinkled, and he tilted his head, continuing to play softly with my aching boner. "Tell me what you'd like, Sport."

"I'd like . . . *this*. Every day," I said, swiping a tear off my cheek. "I want you to use and abuse me and then . . ." My voice cut out, and I couldn't continue.

"And then tell you you're a good boy," Uncle Zach finished for me, nodding like he was in complete agreement. With a smile, he licked up the side of my cock, his eyes on mine, then rose up on his elbow, crawling forward to slip his tongue between my lips as his hand jerked my cock swiftly. I moaned into him, my hands locked around his shoulders as he led the kiss, his free hand cupping the back of my neck as he tongued me deep, the breath in our lungs shared. I whimpered, moving my hips to match his strokes, and then let out a muffled yell as he quickly brought me past the point of oblivion. I broke the kiss, twitching and gasping in his embrace as his palm grew slippery with cum, his hand growing gentler as my dick pushed out one last big spurt, the rest dribbling out weakly as the pulses in my groin slowed and finally stopped.

I couldn't remember the last person who'd made me cum before Uncle Zach. With others, getting jerked or sucked off always felt sort of *forced* on my part. It was like I wasn't fully there in the moment, and the orgasm was just sort of... meh, and disappointing. I hated that feeling, so I just avoided it and took care of myself.

But with my uncle? It felt so natural. No... *more* than natural. It felt familiar. It felt *real*.

I lay there, chest heaving, staring at nothing, trying to catch my breath. Then, his smiling face came back into focus, and all I could think was that he was absolutely fucking perfect and that I was already helplessly, absolutely *crazy* in love with him.

Crazy? No kidding—he's my fucking uncle. I pressed the heels of my hands against my eyes and let out a long, shuddering breath.

"What are we going to do?" I said hoarsely, not really expecting an answer.

"We're going to grab some blankets, curl up on the couch downstairs, and watch a movie. That's what we're going to do," he said, sidestepping the elephant in the room. "And order something to eat . . . though I have to bribe them to come out this far." Uncle Zach leaned in to kiss me softly on the lips. "How does that sound, Sport?"

I smiled.

UNCLE ZACH LET me pick both the movie (*What We Do in the Shadows*) and supper (pasta pomodoro, no cheese . . . just in case my uncle needed my ass again soon) and treated me to a little more of his special soothing cream while we waited for the food to arrive. He had two fingers inside me, massaging my prostate and making me squirm when the doorbell rang. Uncle Zach ran to the door naked and pushed the intercom button.

"Hey, buddy, you can leave it there. Thanks," he said, retrieving the bag on the front step once he was sure the car was gone.

"What's with the intercom thing? How come you don't have, like, smart home speaker thingies and a Ring doorbell?"

Uncle Zach laughed, pulling out the takeaway containers from the bag and grabbing cutlery before joining me on the couch.

"Well, this place was built back in the mid-seventies when structural expressionism was all the rage. But the guy who commissioned it must have watched *The Party* one too many times. The whole place was filled with weird gadgets and like . . . there was a wall right here"—he pointed to the middle of the large living room space—"that came out from over there and unfolded like an accordion. And there was an elevator in the corner, but it opened outside on the patio—bizarre stuff. I had a lot of it taken out when I moved in here; most of the wiring was shot anyway, but I ended up leaving in the intercoms. Dunno. Just handy, I guess."

I nodded.

"Actually, there are a few more things I left in which I think you'll like . . . but I'll show you later."

"Oh yeah?" I grinned.

He kissed me lightly on the lips. "Now, eat your food."

AFTER SUPPER, I lay in my uncle's lap while he played with my hair. I don't think I'd ever felt so safe and warm and perfectly at ease with someone before. I closed my eyes, sighing happily as he scratched my scalp and massaged the back of my neck.

"This is nice," I murmured.

"Mmhm," was all he said, sounding distant. Then he cleared his throat. "Actually, uh, could you move a sec? I have to take a leak."

I sat up, pausing the movie to watch his pert backside disappear down the hallway. I frowned, chewing the corner of my lip. I couldn't help but feel like I was maybe overstaying my welcome, and he was just putting up with me. No, that couldn't be. Not the way he was looking at me earlier. But . . .

Argh.

Was I just another fuckpuppet to him? Did he actually feel something for me? I wouldn't know unless I asked, but I was too afraid to. *Chicken shit.*

"What's with the long face?" Uncle Zach asked, and I looked up and smiled.

"Nothing," I said, forcing a cheerful tone. "Just thinking about stuff."

"Stuff, eh?" he asked, settling on the couch beside me.

"Yeah, just . . . stuff." I shrugged and turned to lay back down in his lap like before, but he had me wait until he scooted down a bit, making me lie on his stomach instead of his thighs.

"That okay?"

I nodded. His dick was right in front of my face, smelling faintly of soap as if he'd just washed it. I guessed he wanted me to suck his cock.

"You sure? You comfortable?"

"Yup."

"Okay. Open your mouth."

I chuckled—I totally called it—and did as I was told. Uncle Zach pushed his soft cock into my mouth, and I immediately began stroking it with my tongue, but my uncle squeezed my shoulder.

"No. You don't need to do anything. I just want you to hold my dick in your mouth."

Oh. A little confused, I stopped trying to get him hard and lay there with his limp cock nestled against my tongue. I swallowed and, in doing so, accidentally sucked on it a little.

"Sorry," I said around Uncle Zach's dick, trying to hold still.

His hands were back in my hair, on my nape—fingers trailing down the length of my spine to cup my backside and back up again to trace the rim of my ear. He stroked my cheek, and I closed my eyes.

"I think it's a natural reaction to want to suckle. Go ahead, but you don't have to get me off. I just like having you keep my dick warm."

I smiled, shifting my head a bit to get more comfortable, and accepted my role as cockwarmer. Uncle Zach pulled the soft blanket up to cover me and hit *play*.

In no time, it felt perfectly natural to watch a movie and laugh with my mouth full of cock.

"Ready?"

I nodded, wondering what he was going to show me. We were lying side by side on the bed, tucked under the crisp white sheets with the lights off. I heard him messing around with something on the headboard; then, a switch clicked. A second later, there was a low hum and a quiet squeak, and I gasped in surprise as the ceiling seemed to slide away. The sky above was a deep blue-black, awash with what looked like a million stars.

"Wow," I whispered. I was a city boy through and through—I don't think I'd ever been this far from the city's light pollution in my life. The night sky was beautiful . . . and humbling.

"Pretty cool, eh?" Uncle Zach asked, turning on his side to watch my reaction to the stars. "I'm glad it's such a clear night. The effect isn't quite as dazzling when it's cloudy."

"I can imagine. Wow," I repeated. "It's like having your own personal planetarium."

"Yup." Uncle Zach reached over and put an arm around me, dragging me closer so he could nuzzle my neck. "When I first bought the place, the mechanism was broken, so I didn't even know what the switches in the bedroom did. I was blown away when I finally figured it out. I had my electrician move all the controls to the headboard here for easy access."

"Is it open to the sky? How do you keep the mosquitos out?"

"No, it's glass. If it was open, we'd have more than mosquitos to worry about. Sometimes there's a whole family of squirrels running around up there."

I laughed, then gasped as my uncle nipped my earlobe gently.

"Owen?" his voice was a low murmur in my ear.

"Yes, Uncle Zach?"

"I'm glad you're here."

"Me too."

FIVE
LOTS OF FIRSTS

I WOKE up as I was being penetrated. I yelled out, but a hand quickly covered my mouth, stifling my cries. Confused, afraid, and not completely awake yet, I pushed back against the body behind me. The cock breaching my hole was like a hot bar of iron, sinking mercilessly into my guts as I helplessly struggled.

Only when he had hilted himself completely did I realize what was happening and forced myself to relax.

"*There* you are, Sport," Uncle Zach said quietly, freeing my mouth.

"Holy shit," I said, my heart hammering. "What a way to wake up."

My uncle chuckled, fucking me with short strokes, keeping his pelvis pressed against my backside.

"I told you. When I said your hole is mine to fuck whenever I want, I was serious."

"Obviously," I whispered, squeezing my eyes shut.

Uncle Zach must have heard something in my tone because he stopped thrusting and propped himself up on one elbow, resting his chin on my bicep. I glanced over, but all I could see was a vague silhouette of his head.

"Did I cross a line?"

I thought about it for a bit. I wasn't entirely sure how I felt about being fucked while still unconscious. Either I was incredibly turned on, as my stiffening dick seemed to be saying, or my fight or flight reflexes had kicked in, and I was *scared*, not turned on. Maybe it was both. *What's wrong with both?*

"I don't know."

"Do you want me to stop?"

I grabbed his hip as he started to pull out and shook my head, holding him inside me.

"No. It's okay. I'm still a little sore, but you feel good. At least now that I know some rando is not raping me in my sleep. I just . . . kinda forgot where I was, that's all."

"Owen. If I screwed up, tell me."

"It's okay, really. I promise." And I wasn't lying. The more I thought about it, the more I was turned on by the fact that my uncle would use me that way. "Look." I took his hand and placed it on my boner.

"Mm," Uncle Zach said, then he surprised me by rolling over on top of me to pin me facedown beneath him. He shifted to sit up and straddle my hips with his dick still lodged inside me, his hands spreading my ass cheeks as he started fucking my hole super slow. "Christ, I can't get enough of you."

"Yeah?" I said, gasping as his thumbs massaged the rim of my stretched-out sphincter against his thick shaft.

"*Fuck*, yeah." His dick throbbed inside me, and he paused, waited a few seconds, and resumed. It seemed like he was going to cum any second now.

"You can do it again. You know, next time I sleep over," I said quietly, hoping there *would* be a next time.

He paused again, but I couldn't tell if it was because he was about to blow his load or because of what I had said.

"Really?" asked Uncle Zach; he sounded relieved.

"Yup. Really." I laughed. "But, I mean, you do like some weird shit."

"I know. I'm sorry."

"No . . . I'm totally here for it," I said, shrugging. I glanced over my shoulder at the dark shadow above me. "No one's ever fucked me in my sleep before. Actually, no one's ever pissed *in* me before today either."

"Heh. Lots of firsts." He chuckled softly and resumed fucking me at the same leisurely pace as before, but it wasn't for long because he had to stop again. "Fuck," he murmured, breathing heavily. He kneaded my cheeks, not moving his dick. "You know what? I want to do something to make it official."

I couldn't breathe for a second, thinking he was talking about a relationship.

"Want to make *what* official?" I asked cautiously.

"That I *literally* own your ass."

"Like a free-use contract?" I laughed, wiggling my hips back and forth, hoping he'd start fucking me again.

"More than that . . ." Uncle Zach huffed out a few breaths and slid his cock nearly out before slamming it into me. "*Oof.* I mean, day or night, your hole is open to me, no matter what."

"Uh-huh." I gasped as he gave another deep thrust. "Sure."

"*And* your boy pussy is mine to give out to *anyone* who wants it."

I moaned at the thought. "Oh god." My throbbing dick slid through a slippery puddle of precum every time he moved. It wouldn't be long before I made a complete mess of his sheets.

"I'm going to take you out to a parking lot and tie you up and blindfold you, and I'm going to charge five bucks a pop to breed your sloppy whore cunt. How does that sound?"

"Oh fuck." I panted. "Yes, please."

"Yeah, you'd fucking love that, wouldn't you, you little slut?"

"Yesss," I whispered, shifting my pelvis back and up to meet his thrusts.

"You'll be tied spread eagle like a helpless bitch, and they'll be lined up around the block, just dying to fill your hole. And I'll be standing there watching you take cock after cock until your ass is so fucking blown out, I can stick a fist in you. Would you like that? A big cum-covered fist for your wrecked hole?"

"Yes. *Please.*" I whimpered, then rasped out a breath as he suddenly leaned hard into his thrusts. His cock hammered my insides, the thick head of it raking past my sweet spot and making my dick spasm in response, faster and faster, until I couldn't hold back my cries. He yelled, flooding my pulsing hole with cum as I jerked and gasped through another powerful orgasm.

Once again, I was crying, with big hiccupping sobs as the throbbing subsided, and he laughed softly, gently taking me into his embrace until my tears ran dry.

"This never happens to me," I said, my breath hitching. "I never cry like this. I'm sorry."

"Don't be," Uncle Zach said, his gaze warm. He brought his mouth to mine and kissed me so sweetly that I thought I would start bawling again. "I love that I can take you apart like this."

I rubbed my face, embarrassed but sort of weirdly proud. "And put me back together."

Uncle Zach chuckled. "That too." Then he sighed and looked up. The sky was beginning to lighten—no wonder I could see him now. "Okay. Time to sleep, Sport," he said and touched a button. The panel slowly crept across the ceiling until the room was dark again.

To avoid the large wet spot I'd left on the sheets, I had to move closer to my uncle, which was nothing to complain about. I curled up against his back, one arm around his waist. My body and mind were exhausted—it would take no time to fall asleep.

As I was starting to drift off, Uncle Zach spoke up, startling me.

"I know what we'll do. We'll go to my buddy's tattoo place in town tomorrow—that is, if you don't have plans."

"Hm? No plans. Why?" I asked, blinking sleepily.

"Because he's going to tattoo ZC on your ass."

"ZC?"

"Zachary Cunningham. That'll make it official."

"Oh," I said, laughing quietly as I closed my eyes. "Seriously?"

"Dead serious."

"Why only ZC? Why not tattoo 'Uncle Zach's Fuckhole' with an arrow pointing down," I said, only half joking.

Uncle Zach was silent for a while.

"You'd do that?" he asked finally.

I opened my eyes, staring at the tattoos on his back that were barely visible in the darkness.

"Yeah. I would," I replied at length, thinking I'd do almost anything for him at that point. "You could also get my name tattooed on you too. Somewhere."

"Sure, Sport." He didn't say anything else, and I thought he'd fallen asleep, but just as I was drifting off again, I thought I heard him say, "*Fuck*, what am I doing?"

SIX
LIOR COMES HOME

I woke up alone again in Uncle Zach's bed. The room was dark, and it looked like my uncle didn't own an alarm clock, so I had no idea what time it was. I felt around on the headboard for the switch that controlled the ceiling cover, but there was a whole bunch.

"Eenie, meenie, miney, mo," I said, picking one. I flicked it, but to my disappointment, nothing happened. I wondered if it used to control one of the weird gadgets my uncle had mentioned removing. I tried the next switch, which did nothing too, but the third one I tried slid the blackout curtains away from the patio doors. I shielded my eyes and got out of bed, walking to the doors to see if my uncle was outside. The lounge chairs were empty, but I noticed he'd removed the cover from the hot tub.

Sweet.

"Owen?" Uncle Zach's voice crackled from the intercom. "You up?"

I ran over and hit the switch. "Yup."

"I *thought* I heard something. Come on down. I made waffles."

My stomach gurgled, and I grinned. "Be right there." I started putting on my shorts but remembered what he had said the day before about wanting me naked at all times, so I left them on the floor next to the bed and went downstairs for breakfast in the buff.

"How'd you sleep?" Uncle Zach asked and gave me a quick kiss like we were a real couple.

"Really well." I smiled when he squeezed my ass gently. "You?"

A tiny frown flickered across his face, and I remembered what he'd said as I was falling asleep.

"I slept okay."

"You all right?"

He sighed and lifted one shoulder in a slight shrug. "I dunno." Uncle Zach pointed to one of the stools. "Sit."

I sat down, and he placed a plate of strawberry-covered waffles in front of me, but I didn't pick up my fork.

"Tell me what's wrong." I reached out to take his hand.

"We shouldn't be doing this," he said, looking down at his hand in mine.

"Why? We're not hurting anyone."

"Not *yet*. Can you imagine what would happen if my brother found out I fucked his son? Shit. He might never talk to me again. And I don't want that to happen. I love Teddy."

"How is anyone going to find out?"

"If we get too comfortable . . . even doing something little like this," he said, squeezing my hand. "There's a chance that we'll forget ourselves and do it in public. Do you know how hard it'll be for me to keep my hands off you?"

I nodded. "I know. But if we're *really* careful . . ."

"I think we need to nip this in the bud, Sport." He slid his hand out of mine. "It's for the best."

"No."

"It's an impossible situation." He shook his head. "It never should have happened."

"But it did, and I don't want it to stop."

"Owen, be reasonable. How can we possibly . . ." Uncle Zach sighed again, rubbing his face. "Listen, when I woke up this morning with you in my bed, I felt so fucking happy. Like I was the luckiest guy in the world."

My heart thudded in my chest as my cheeks grew warm. "You did?" I whispered.

"Yes. And then I thought, shit, how the hell am I going to keep that off my face? One look, and anyone will be able to tell that I'm crazy about you."

"You are?"

"Isn't it obvious?" he asked, his brows high, then he shook his head, running both hands through his hair. "Argh. This is so fucking *wrong*."

"I don't think it's wrong," I said quietly, my heart in my throat. "Don't end this . . . please?"

Uncle Zach stared at me, the muscles bunching in his jaw, then he exhaled hard and went down on his knees in front of me, resting his cheek on my knee. I smoothed out his hair as he stayed there with his eyes closed, a wrinkle on his brow.

"We can make it work," I said.

"How?" My uncle opened his eyes, lifting his head.

I shrugged. "We'll figure it out as we go." I parted my knees so I could draw him closer, and he nuzzled my stomach, pressing a trail of soft kisses down to my dick. Then he looked up at me again, rubbing his lips against the side of my hardening shaft.

"I don't *want* this to stop," he murmured. "Believe me. But we can't go on like this."

"You're being awfully dramatic."

Uncle Zach gave a little chuckle. I put my hand under his chin to raise his head and leaned down to kiss him. Coaxing his lips open, I gently slid my tongue against his, entwining them, and he let out a moan. I smiled into the kiss and then released him.

"I saw you took the cover off the hot tub," I said.

A crease appeared between his brows. "I did. I was going to suggest a soak later, but now my head is all—"

"Stop it. We're going to eat breakfast, and then we'll get in the hot tub, and you're going to fuck me."

Smirking, Uncle Zach sat back on his heels. "Am I, now?"

"You are," I said, grabbing my fork. "That's an order."

"Yes, sir," he replied, looking amused as he got to his feet. I watched him walk back to the waffle maker and sighed. He was right, of course. Short of moving far away from anyone who knew us, our relationship was completely unfeasible, no matter what we felt for each other. But I didn't want to dwell on it and cast a shadow over the day ahead. We could pretend that everything would be fine for just a little longer.

UNCLE ZACH HUFFED A FEW BREATHS, his hands on my hips, holding me down while his dick throbbed in my tender hole. I clenched my ass and wiggled a little, eliciting another moan from my uncle, then draped my arms around his neck, pulling him in for a kiss. We'd been at it for a good half hour—I'd brought him right to the edge of climax probably a dozen times, but he always stopped me when he was too close.

"Fuck, you feel good on my cock," he said, releasing me to run his hands up my back. I rose on my knees and started riding his dick again slowly, my hands on his shoulders to keep my balance. My boner bobbed up and down in the warm water, the currents caused by my movements teasing the sensitive head. I was getting close too.

The sound of the patio door startled me, and I turned, my heart racing.

"Hey, man," said the stranger, walking up to the hot tub.

"Lior! Didn't hear you pull up," replied Uncle Zach cheerfully.

"I guess you were a little distracted, eh?" said Lior, grinning at us. My face felt like it was on fire. *This* was Lior? He wasn't at all what I expected.

My uncle's roommate-cum-housekeeper was tall and thin, with shoulder length wavy black hair, and a thick moustache. His deep tan was set off by the white linen shirt he wore unbuttoned, and his lean chest and flat belly were covered in a sparse thicket of black fur. Around his neck, he had a gold chain with a little Star of David pendant.

Letting my gaze fall, I saw his jeans were tight enough that his dick was clearly outlined and that he was barefoot. The most surprising thing, however, was his age. I figured he was in his late forties or early fifties—the hair at his temples was greying. I'd assumed Lior would be the same age as Uncle Zach, maybe younger. I seriously couldn't imagine him and my uncle fucking, even if he *was* handsome in a 70's hippy sort of way. But . . . who fucked who? I had taken my uncle to be a hundred percent top—now I wasn't so sure.

"Lior, this is Owen. Owen, Lior," Uncle Zach said nonchalantly like I wasn't straddling his lap, his dick buried to the balls in my ass.

"Your nephew?" Lior asked, dipping his hand into the hot tub like he was checking the temperature. He gave us a lopsided grin, his mouth all but disappearing under his moustache. "Kinky." I had the distinct impression that very little shocked Lior.

"Care to join us?"

My eyes snapped back to my uncle, startled, and he smiled serenely at me. Join us for *what*?

"Love to," Lior replied, and I turned to watch him shrug off his shirt and drop it on the ground. Like my uncle, his nipples were pierced, but where Uncle Zach had barbells through his, Lior had small, thick rings. Uncle Zach took me by the waist, making me move on his dick again while Lior peeled off his jeans. He had no underwear on, and when he straightened, my eyes widened at the sight of the big Prince Albert piercing in his cockhead. Without a word, he stepped into the hot tub, settling on the bench across from us so I had my back to him.

I kept riding my uncle's cock slowly, feeling Lior's eyes on me. Plenty of guys had watched me fuck, but this was weird and intimate. I was turned on . . . but I was also a little freaked out.

"How's your mom?" Uncle Zach asked Lior.

"Oh, she's fine. She got her eyes lasered a few weeks ago. Weird seeing her without those coke bottles, you know?"

He and my uncle began chatting like I wasn't even there. Sometimes Uncle Zach would stop me for a few seconds or make me move faster, but other than his touches, he completely ignored me. I couldn't decide if I liked what was happening or not, and my mind kept returning to the fact that he and Lior were fuck buddies.

Didn't he just tell you this morning he was crazy about you? I chided myself. As if hearing my thoughts, Uncle Zach turned his focus on me and pecked a kiss on my lips.

"I gotta hit the john," he said, then looked over my shoulder at Lior. "Wanna keep his hole warm for me?"

"Sure, gimme a sec," Lior replied.

"*What?*" I asked, startled.

My uncle's grin got sly. "Whose hole is it?"

I let out a nervous laugh. "Yeah . . . but . . ."

"No buts. Go on now." He lifted me off his lap, his dick popping free of my ass. My pucker hung open for a moment, and the water filling my hole felt slightly cooler than my insides. I stayed on my knees, watching my uncle climb out of the hot tub, then I took a deep breath and turned shyly to Lior. He was jerking his dick, making it hard, and he motioned for me to approach.

I thought for a second that he would ask me to suck his dick, but he just grabbed me around the waist and lifted me. I straddled him like I had been doing with my uncle and let myself sink onto his pierced cock.

Lior let out a pleased moan, then smiled at me.

"You're a good-looking kid, you know that?"

"Uh. Thanks," I said, embarrassed. I averted my gaze as I started riding Lior, wondering when my uncle would return.

"I can see the family resemblance."

"Yeah?"

"For sure—you guys could be brothers. Here . . . stay put. I'll do the work." He surprised me by wrapping his wiry arms around me, pulling me against his furry chest, then he buried his face in my neck, holding onto me tight as he lifted his pelvis, fucking his cock up into me as I braced myself on my knees. His moustache tickled my neck, but in a nice way, and he smelled great. I decided right then that I liked Lior.

It wasn't long before I heard the patio door again.

"Hey, man," Lior said, sitting up. "Want him back?"

"Did you cum in him yet?" asked Uncle Zach.

"Wasn't sure if I oughta."

"Go on and finish. I'll wait . . . I can use your load as lube."

Lior chuckled, then gave me another of his crooked grins. I liked how his green eyes crinkled at the corners when he smiled.

"Then we'd better get out," he said to me.

"Oh. Why?" I asked. I liked the feel of the water on my skin as I was fucked.

"Who do you think'll have to clean up the mess in the hot tub?" He pointed to his chest with his thumb. "This guy."

With his help, I got out of the water and went down on all fours on the deck. Lior promptly impaled me with his cock again. His shaft was thinner and shorter than my uncle's, but the thick metal ring was hitting my prostate in *just* the right way—a puddle of precum was growing between my knees.

"Open up," Uncle Zach said, pointing his dick at my mouth.

I started sucking my uncle's cock, balancing on one hand to fondle his balls while Lior pounded away at my hole. It wasn't long before Lior's thrusts started to slow, and then he startled me by letting out a yell and going still as his dick twitched deep in my ass. I pulled Uncle Zach's cock out of my mouth to look over my shoulder just as Lior threw back his head and let out a howl. I couldn't help my laughter. What a weirdo.

Lior grinned at me, winked, then slapped my ass.

"Thanks, kid," he said, getting to his feet. He swept up his jeans and shirt and walked to the patio door in the nude. His narrow ass was as brown as the rest of him—no doubt he took full advantage of my uncle's secluded patio to sunbathe naked. "Shall I make something for lunch?" Lior asked, pausing in the doorway as he looked back.

"Nah, we had a late breakfast," Uncle Zach replied. He motioned for me to get on my back on the deck. Kneeling between my spread thighs, he used his thumbs to pull my ass open, biting his lip as he shook his head. "Oh, that's nice." I could feel a glob of warm cum run down my crack to the boards beneath me.

"What about supper?"

"Sure. Whatever you feel like," my uncle replied. He grabbed my wrists and pulled them above my head, holding them down with one hand as he positioned his cock with the other.

"Owen, you like quinoa?" asked Lior.

"Uh. Sh-sure," I replied, distracted by my uncle rubbing his cockhead against my hole. Then I cried out when Uncle Zach suddenly hilted himself inside me. Lior laughed as he closed the patio door, and we were alone again.

Uncle Zach stared down at me as he pulled back and rammed himself to the balls again, shifting to hold my wrists with both hands now. I whimpered, wrapping my legs around his hips.

"Jesus, I love fucking your sloppy cunt," he said, his brow deeply furrowed as he fucked me slow and deep, the thick head of his cock raking my prostate and making my boner jerk up from my belly. "How's that feel?"

I moaned in reply and soon found myself gasping in time with his thrusts.

"I'm . . ." I whispered, taking a shaky breath and trying again. "I'm . . . getting close. Oh my god, I'm going to cum."

"That's right, Sport," my uncle said, smiling. "Your hole just loves your uncle's big dick, doesn't it?"

I nodded, squeezing my eyes shut.

"Cum for me. I want to feel you cum on my dick before I fill that whore cunt with another load. You can do it . . . cum for me. Yeah, that's it . . . *good* boy. Cum for your Uncle Zach."

Panting, I tightened my legs around him, pulling him into me deep as the first pulse of orgasm hit me. The yell I let out as I came was so loud that my voice echoed over the lake, and as I took in another breath to moan my pleasure, Uncle Zach covered my mouth with his, kissing me hard as his cock throbbed and spurted inside me, breeding my hole again. When his dick gave a last twitch, I shuddered and gasped, wrapping my arms around him when he let go of my wrists to collapse on top of me, breathing hard.

Nuzzling my neck softly, he murmured, "Mmm. That was nice."

There was no way we could end this. We were too perfect together.

SEVEN
BREAKING THE DAM

WE LAY there in the midday sun, the cool breeze drying the water and sweat from our skin, and despite my best efforts at keeping still, my uncle's limp cock eventually slid out of me. I sighed, and he rolled over with a chuckle.

"Come on," he said, sitting up. He held out a hand to me as he stood—I assumed he was leading us to the bathroom so I could wash the cum off my belly, but instead, he pointed at the bed.

"Uh," I said, frowning. "What are we doing?"

"I'm not done with you yet," he said with a sly grin.

"What do you mean?" I asked, sitting on the edge of the bed. I nervously watched him search through the drawer in the wardrobe. "I don't think I can go again." My balls ached, and my ass was throbbing in time with my heartbeat.

"Nonsense," he replied, holding aloft a dark grey toy. It resembled the prostate massager he'd used on me before, but it was thicker and longer and had a power cord with a small black remote attached. "I think you've got it in you to cum again, Sport, and this'll do the trick."

"What is it?" I asked, eyes wide as he came around to plug it into an outlet on the headboard.

"You'll see."

"I don't . . ."

"Trust me." He brushed his hair back from his forehead and gave me such an endearing smile that I begrudgingly humoured him when he had me lie on my back with my knees up. Uncle Zach then lay beside me and lubed up the toy before gently inserting it into my ass. I winced, but it wasn't that bad, just a little uncomfortable.

"Now what?" I asked. "I really don't think I can . . ."

"You can and you will," my uncle replied, touching the remote. The toy came alive in my hole, vibrating but not swirling like the prostate massager. "How's that?"

"It's okay," I replied, doubtful that the vibrations could make me have another orgasm, then he hit another switch on the remote, and my whole body twitched. "Oh!"

Laughing, Uncle Zach watched me jerk in place when the toy kept zapping my prostate.

"*Fuuck*," I gasped. It was unlike anything I'd ever felt. The combination of vibrations and electricity had my dick drooling over my stomach in seconds. "Oh, my god."

"Should I turn it up?" he asked but didn't wait for my reply before upping the speed and force of the shocks.

"Oh. Oh. *Oh*." I couldn't stop crying out. My dick wasn't even hard, but without a doubt, the toy inside me would force me to cum. I gasped as my uncle took my soft, slippery cock in hand, jerking it slowly—in no time, my dick and balls were completely soaked from the precum leaking out of me in a continuous stream.

"Do you like it?"

"I... oh *oh*... oh *god*," I said, uncertain. "Yes? I don't know." There were so many sensations inside me that it took me a moment to realize that my bladder was crying out for attention. "I *oh*... I think I have to pee. Shit. *Shit*, oh *god*."

"So do it," Uncle Zach said with a little shrug, but when he didn't shut off the e-stim toy and kept playing with my cock, I realized he had no intention of stopping so I could use the bathroom. That could only mean he meant—

I gaped at him. "What? *Here*?"

"Sure. Why not? The mattress pad is waterproof, and the sheets *really* need changing anyway, so . . . go ahead. Let loose."

Startled, I could only stare at him, my hips still bucking with every shock to my prostate. He sat up to take my dick in both hands and concentrated on my piss-hole, rubbing it quickly with his thumb.

"Come on, Sport. It's all right."

I whimpered, the urge to piss mounting as he stimulated my slit.

"I can't," I whispered, tears filling my eyes.

"You *can*," Uncle Zach said gently.

"I can't." But by then, I couldn't hold back anymore, and I *did*.

Moaning, I held my eyes closed as I lay there pissing in my uncle's bed, all over my uncle's hand as he stroked me softly, directing my stream downwards so that it didn't arc in the air, keeping the puddle confined to the bed. I was amazed by how utterly *freeing* it was to be given permission to pee myself, and the pleasure I felt having my cock handled while doing it was intense. Suddenly, I couldn't tell when my pissing had ended and my orgasm had begun—my balls and my prostate were nearly empty, and my dick was still soft, but I let out a cry as I came so hard that the toy was squeezed out of my ass, my body convulsing through at least a dozen, teeth clenching contractions. When it was over, I lay there in a daze, panting. I buzzed from head to toe, and I was covered in goosebumps.

What just happened?

Uncle Zach smiled wide. "See? What did I tell you?"

My mind was so blitzed that I couldn't form words. I just blinked slowly at him.

"Come on," he said, taking my hand. With his help, I walked on jellied legs to the bathroom where he had me sit on the far side of the huge shower stall while he readied the water.

"Okay, it'll take a second to warm up—" He stopped and frowned when he saw my expression. "Owen?"

The dam broke.

I began to cry. Big ugly sobs shook my body and made it hard to breathe. I was overwhelmed. I felt lost inside myself and confused and ashamed, and I didn't even know why I was crying. Uncle Zach quickly went down on his knees in front of me and pulled me into a hug, and the harder he squeezed me, the harder I cried. He dragged me under the warm, simulated rainfall and coaxed me to lie down, then he curled up behind me and wrapped his arms around me while he whispered words of comfort.

"That's it. Let it all out. It's okay. I'm here. You're safe . . ." Uncle Zach then did something that surprised me and brought me back a little to myself. He slipped his half-hard cock into me gently—not to fuck me, just to be *inside* me, connected.

We lay there for a long time, the gentle water rinsing the sweat and cum and piss down the drain along with my tears. Eventually, I stopped shaking when my sobs had run their course, and all that was left was a profound sense of serenity.

"Wow."

"You okay?" my uncle asked, kissing the back of my neck.

"Yeah. More than okay," I replied. "I am *so* zen right now." My body felt light as a feather.

Uncle Zach chuckled, then groaned as I shifted in place—the tiles under my hip were getting less comfortable by the minute.

"Um . . . I'm going to cum if you move again," he said, his voice hoarse.

It was then that I realized that at some point during my crying jag, my uncle's dick had gotten fully hard, and he was now skirting the edge despite us lying mostly still.

"What, you don't want to?" I asked, smiling.

"Well . . . I wasn't sure how you'd feel about it," he replied. "The um . . . timing didn't seem appropriate. Didn't feel right blowing my load while you were still crying like that."

I chuckled, eliciting another moan from him, and said, "Go ahead."

He gasped, then bit down on my shoulder gently, pushing his hips into me as he came, his body shuddering against mine.

"Oh, thank fucking god," he said, nuzzling the back of my neck again when he was done. "Oof. I've been on the edge for at *least* ten minutes. I was starting to think I was just going to have to hide the fact that I was cumming."

"You're funny." I twined my fingers with his and sighed, closing my eyes. His softening dick felt nice inside me. "How are you so good at this?"

"Good at what?"

"Knowing exactly what I need when I don't even know it myself."

"Ah."

He was quiet for a long time, so I squeezed his hand.

"What are you thinking about?" I asked.

"You."

I thought I would burst into tears again, my chest got so tight at the affection in his voice. I had a zillion butterflies in my stomach as I nervously opened my mouth to speak.

Will I regret it?

"Uncle Zach?"

"Yeah?"

"I love you." I felt him stiffen at my words and held my breath, filled with hope and dread as I waited for him to speak.

"Christ, Owen," he said, sounding a little hoarse. "*Fuck.*"

Startled, I pulled away from him to turn around. He was frowning with his eyes closed and was pinching the bridge of his nose between his sandy brows.

I sat up, my heart beating so hard I could feel it through my whole body.

"I'm sorry," I said in a small voice.

Uncle Zach's eyes snapped open, and he shook his head.

"No... *no*," he said, smiling as he lifted himself off the tiles. His eyes were red. "Don't be sorry, Sport. You've just got *me* crying now, is all." He chuckled, swiping at his cheek. "What a fucking mess, eh? Shit, what the hell are we going to do?" He reached out to cup my cheek, and I leaned into his touch, confused. "I've never been in love before," he said softly.

"No?" My speeding pulse was making me lightheaded. What was he trying to say?

"No." His smile became a little shy. "But now I know what it feels like."

"Oh." We sat there just staring into each other's eyes for a second, then he actually blushed before looking away.

"Okay, enough of this sappy stuff, eh?" Uncle Zach chucked me lightly on the chin. "What do you say we go see what Lior's cooking up for supper? Hm?"

Euphoric doesn't begin to cover what I felt knowing my uncle was in love with me. I was giddy and beaming from ear to ear as he helped me to my feet. We began to wash up but got sidetracked when my little kiss of affection turned into a lengthy make-out session. By the time we were finally rinsing off, the water was barely lukewarm.

I WAS SURPRISED to see that the bed was made—the sheets had obviously been replaced, and two fluffy black robes were waiting for us.

"That Lior's a good man," Uncle Zach said, scrubbing his hair with a towel.

My cheeks were hot, and my embarrassment must have been written all over my face because my uncle frowned.

"What's wrong?"

"He's going to think I peed the bed," I whispered, mortified.

"Well . . . you *did*." He laughed.

"I know, but . . . that was an *us* thing, you know? I didn't think Lior would have to clean up my mess. Oh god. I can't go down there."

"Relax, Sport," Uncle Zach said, squeezing my towel-covered backside. "Lior doesn't care. I promise it's fine." He chuckled at my expression and shook his head. "Listen, if you're that embarrassed, I'll just say I'm the one who pissed myself. Okay?"

"Ugh." I covered my face as my uncle put his hands on my shoulders.

"Owen, look at me."

Sighing, I dropped my hands and met his gaze.

"Lior doesn't give a shit about that kind of thing. *Trust* me." He tugged on the towel around my hips, letting it fall to the floor so he could grab my bare ass and pull me against him. "Besides," he said, sliding his cool fingers down my crack to stroke my sore pucker gently, "do you *really* think this is the first time Lior's cleaned a boy's piss out of my bed? Hm?"

I frowned.

Laughing, he leaned forward and pecked a chaste kiss on my forehead before releasing me. "There, now you're jealous instead of embarrassed," he said, flicking me with his towel.

"Ouch. No, now I'm jealous *and* embarrassed."

"Aw." Grinning, he tied his robe. "Poor kiddo."

"And you're mean."

Uncle Zach bit his bottom lip, tilting his head at me, a solemn expression on his face.

"What?" I asked, shrugging on the other robe.

"I just . . . I really like this. You . . . Me." He sighed. "I'm happy, you know?"

I smiled. "Yeah?"

"Yeah." He pulled me in for a soft kiss, then leaned back, his brow wrinkled. "I never even asked if you were staying over again tonight. Are you?"

"Will you have me?"

"Of course," Uncle Zach replied, a mischievous smile dimpling his handsome face. "Hopefully, at least twice before bed."

SUPPER WAS tasty even though I couldn't really tell what it was that I was eating. Lior was a vegetarian and cooked what my mother would call "crunchy-granola food," but I had no complaints. And Uncle Zach was right—Lior didn't bring up the soiled sheets once, though it seemed like he had a knowing glint in his eye when we'd finally come downstairs.

After we ate, Uncle Zach and I took to the couch to watch *Fear and Loathing in Las Vegas*. Lior had eaten an edible about an hour earlier and was "grooving," as he put it, and went to his room to listen to music.

"Why don't you lie down like you did yesterday?" Uncle Zach asked, opening his robe. I grinned and curled up on my side, my head on my uncle's belly with his soft cock in my mouth and his hand stroking my hair.

"Thank you," he said quietly after a few minutes.

At first, I thought he was just thanking me for keeping his dick warm, but the gravity in his tone registered a moment later, and I realized that he was thanking me for *everything*. I sighed, so happy my heart felt full to bursting and ran my tongue gently along his soft shaft for a second. I reached for his free hand and took it in mine.

Life couldn't get more perfect.

EIGHT
TAINT ART

"Ow. *Ow!*" I wailed, clutching the sides of the padded bench I was kneeling on. My face was pressed to the black leather, and my bare ass was up in the air, getting brutally tortured.

"Hey, whose idea was it to get your taint tattooed?" Uncle Zach said, sounding amused. "I suggested ass cheek."

"*Fuck* that hurts," I replied through clenched teeth while Uncle Zach's tattooist friend Brad attacked my sensitive flesh again with his needles. It was like getting stung by a horsefly over and over in the same spot. "How long does it take to tattoo two fucking letters?"

Brad chuckled and paused his work. "You want fast? You get crapola. I'm an artist. This ain't no hack job. Now quit moving."

"Sorry," I said, then gasped as he resumed. Uncle Zach had chosen a fancy gothic font for his initials, which was why it was taking so long, I figured, but he'd let me choose the spot. I'd really wanted his initials to be as close to "his" hole as possible, so my ass cheek wasn't going to cut it. At first, I thought about getting it right above my ass crack, but I'd read somewhere that getting tattooed over bone hurts like hell, and there's not much meat to speak of in that area. So, between my balls and my asshole seemed the right choice.

I didn't regret my decision, though. It was probably the most painful and *humiliating* thing I'd ever gone through . . . but also the most exciting. Just thinking about how he'd be able to see his initials right above his cock while he was fucking me had made my dick hard at first, though I'd gone as limp as could be the minute Brad had started carving into me. I enjoyed pain but not pain like *this*.

Eyes squeezed shut, I tried to hold as still as possible for Brad, the world's slowest tattoo artist. Finally, after what felt like an hour under the gun, Brad stepped back to admire his work.

"All right. I'm done the Z. Gonna take a little break and do the C in a few minutes."

"What?" I said, lifting my head. "You're only half done?" Then I saw the smirks on Brad and Uncle Zach's faces, and I knew they were fucking with me. "Oh, thank god."

"Wanna see?" Brad asked, wiping my taint with a paper towel.

"Yeah."

He spritzed something cool on me, and I squealed, but the cold felt good on my burning skin. He wiped again, then I heard a click.

Brad came around to show me his phone. "You're swollen as all hell, but that'll go down soon. Sitting's not going to be fun for a while, though."

The ZC was upside down, but that was what we'd decided on since it would be right side up when I was on my back, and my skin was red and puffy, but the lines of the tattoo were so crisp and perfect that they looked like they'd been put there by a machine.

"Wow. That looks amazing," I said, smiling at Brad. He grinned back at me and put his phone away.

"See? I do quality work." He laughed, shaking his head. "Not that I'll be able to show it off on my Instagram. Never tattooed a guy's perineum before."

"Is that what it's actually called?"

"Yep." He carefully cut some paper into a circle, and when he was done, he peeled the backing off—I saw that it was a sort of bandage. "Now, hold still. This is second skin… it'll protect the tattoo. Leave it on for a few days, okay?"

"Okay. Thank you." Uncle Zach helped me off the table, and

while I was gingerly pulling my boxers and shorts back up, Brad peeled off his gloves and held his hand out to my uncle.

"Thanks for squeezing us in, Brad," my uncle said as they shook. "Really appreciate it."

"No worries, my man," Brad replied. "Though I think you owe me for making me stare at someone's poop chute for so long." He chuckled, shaking his head again so that his locs swung. "You like some crazy, weird shit."

Uncle Zach clapped his friend on the shoulder and winked. "You don't know the half of it."

SITTING *WAS* UNCOMFORTABLE, and the pain was so distracting that it took me a while to realize we were driving east along the highway, not west.

"Where are we going?" I asked, shifting so that I was putting my weight on my left butt cheek.

"I'm driving you home," he replied as he did a shoulder check and changed lanes.

I stared at him in dismay. "What? *Why?*"

Uncle Zach glanced over at me with a teasing grin, his brow furrowed. "Don't you have like . . . a life to get back to? Plants that need watering? I don't know . . . A job?"

"Nope. My roommates are jerks, I don't have any plants, and school *just* ended. I like taking a few weeks off before looking for a summer job. I've really got nothing going on."

"What about a pair of fresh boxers?" he asked.

"I can wear some of yours. We're the same size." I could hear the pleading in my voice and hated it, but I hated the thought of going home even more. "Besides, you like me naked all the time. Why do I need boxers?"

Uncle Zach laughed, reached over to squeeze my knee, and gave me a serious look.

"Listen . . . just go home for a few days. You know I won't be able to keep my hands off you if I take you back to my place, and you should really take some time to heal. Besides, I'm sure your ass could use a rest."

"But—"

"No buts. I also need to do some work for the upcoming release, and I'm getting absolutely nothing done with you around."

My eyes started to sting, so I turned away to stare out the window. I didn't want him to see I was close to tears. "Sorry."

"Don't be sorry. It's all right." We took the offramp, and I sighed. I'd be home in a few minutes. "Actually . . . *huh* . . . I think you just gave me an idea," he said brightly, and I turned to stare at his profile.

"Oh? An idea for what?"

His smile got sly, and he shook his head.

"I don't want to say anything just yet. There's something I have to do first."

"Give me a hint?"

"Nope."

"Please?"

Uncle Zach shook his head, then turned onto a little side street and killed the engine.

"Why are we stopping here?" I asked, confused. I lived a half dozen or so blocks away.

"Because I want to kiss you, and I don't want your neighbours to see."

"My neighbours don't know you're my uncle," I replied.

"Just being cautious." He curled his hand around the back of my neck and pulled me into a kiss. His tongue sought mine out, teasing me as our mouths moved slowly, lips mashed together almost painfully. It didn't matter how many times we'd kissed—I still got butterflies. However, this was the first time a kiss from him made me sad. It was a goodbye kiss.

I drew back. "I can go home tomorrow."

Uncle Zach pressed his lips together tight and pushed a lock of hair away from my eyes.

"It's only for a few days. I'll come get you Thursday afternoon . . . Okay, Sport?"

I knew I was pouting, but I couldn't help it. "Wednesday."

"No, I have something on Wednesday."

Sighing, I shrugged. "Fine. Thursday morning."

He laughed and shook his head. "All right. Thursday *morning*. And make sure you take good care of that tattoo. Use the ointment Brad gave you. I want you as healed up as possible so that I don't have to worry about it while I'm wrecking your slutty boycunt," he said, putting a growl into his words at the end.

"Oh fuck," I whispered.

Uncle Zach stared hard at me, his nostrils flaring, then I could see the muscles roll in his jaw as he clenched his teeth. With a sharp exhale, he tugged at the crotch of his khakis—evidently, he was getting stiff.

"Hey, does your car have, like, a top?"

"Yeah, why?"

"Would you like to fuck my mouth?"

His eyes widened, and he took a few quick breaths. "Christ, yes." It was almost comical how fast his finger hit the convertible's roof control—his cock was out of his pants before the top had even finished extending.

"Are you sure I can't come home with you?" I tried one last time.

"Shut up and gag on my dick like a good little bitch," Uncle Zach said. Contrary to his words and angry tone, his expression was softly affectionate, and I laughed, leaning over to take his big cock in my mouth. I planned on taking my sweet time with him, of course —anything to extend our time together. Thursday was just *so* far away.

NINE
SENT HOME

WITH THE TASTE of my uncle's cum fresh on my tongue and tears once again brimming in my eyes, I stood there and watched the convertible speed away and turn on the next block. In a blink, Uncle Zach was gone.

Fuck. Sighing, I clenched my jaw and wiped my face with my sleeve before entering the lower duplex I shared with two guys from uni. As I opened the door, I was blasted with the stench of dirty gym socks, and I covered my nose to keep from gagging as I stepped over the pile of old sneakers and random sports equipment in the front hall. Jason and Digger were ultimate dude-bro types—they played rugby and lacrosse in the summer and hockey in the winter, drank beer almost exclusively, had posters of cars and naked chicks in their rooms, and once drew dicks on my face when I had the misfortune of falling asleep in their presence. Thankfully, they didn't go in for homophobic slurs, or I would have moved out long ago. They were jerks, but they didn't care that I was gay. In fact, for all their constant bragging about all the chicks they were "boning," I was almost certain they were fucking each other.

I walked into the living room to find the usual mess of take-out containers, empty beer bottles, and assorted dumbbells and thought about how tidy my uncle's place was in comparison. I sighed and used some wooden take-out chopsticks to move a pair of wrinkled boxers off the couch so I could sit, and was startled by Digger stepping out of Jason's room naked.

"Oh, shit, dude," Digger said, covering his dick with both hands. "I didn't hear you come in. Where you been, man?"

I realized I was staring at his rock-hard abs and big round pecs and cleared my throat, averting my eyes. My roommates might have been dickish pigs, but damn, they were nice to look at.

"I was at my uncle's." *And he was fucking my brains out.* Feeling cheeky about my secret, I glanced up again with a small smile. "Hey . . . Why were you *naked* in Jay's room?" I couldn't help myself.

Digger's face flushed, but to his credit, his expression never changed.

"Just lookin' for some clean boxers," he said, shrugging.

"Mmhmm." I held his gaze, and he shrugged again before turning and presenting me with a view of his furry bubble butt as he retreated to his room. Was that a handprint on his backside?

A moment later, Jason stepped out looking like he had hastily dressed—his dirty blond hair resembled a haystack.

"Hey, man." He stood there a moment, smoothing down his hair with one hand before covering it with his usual ratty blue baseball cap. "Uh, we're outta toilet paper." He turned at a muffled yell coming from Digger's room. "Oh . . . and uh, dish soap."

"Okay?" I stared at him.

"D'you mind um . . . you know?"

I blinked at him slowly. "I wasn't even *here* for *days*, and you want me to go to the store for you?"

"Yeah, d'you mind? Digger n' me were just about to put the game on. Oh, and can you get snacks?" After another unintelligible shout from Digger's room, he added, "And beer?"

"No," I said, wincing as I stepped towards the kitchen.

"What's wrong with you? Get your ass wrecked by a big dick?" Jason let out a chuckle.

"Something like that." My hole felt bruised, sure, but it was the throbbing new tattoo that made it hard to walk.

"Alrighty. You're off the hook, dude."

"Thanks," I muttered, shuffling to the fridge. I opened the freezer and found a bag of frozen corn. I turned as Jason snagged a half-empty beer bottle off the shelf behind the couch, taking a swig. He made a face. "Digger! Get your sweet ass out here and come with me to the Dep. The O-man's got a sore bum, so he won't go to the store."

I shook my head and walked carefully to my room, where I gingerly stripped down to my boxers, then lay back with my knees up and thighs wide, the frozen corn resting against my aching taint while I flipped through my phone. No message from my uncle, but he wouldn't be home yet anyway. However, a second later, an email from him came in with a chime, and I eagerly opened it. There was no message, only a video attachment. Frowning, I clicked on it and quickly turned down the volume. There I was, on all fours, with my uncle's big dick slamming into me.

With a shaky breath, I stared hungrily at the video as Uncle Zach pulled out and spat hard into my gaping hole before mounting me again. I hadn't even realized he was filming us.

I watched the four-minute video, my hand slowly stroking my dick, and was already about to blow my load when another email came in from my uncle. This time there was a message:

Watch it all you like, Sport. Jerk off to it if you want . . . but you're not allowed to cum.

Smirking, I shook my head and started the video over, working my cock again quickly. How would he even know?

Another email came in with a chime, and I glanced at it. It simply said:

I'll know.

I swallowed hard as my pulse raced, squeezing my shaft to ground myself again.

"Shit." I *very* gently released myself and just sat there staring at my dick as it twitched with my heartbeat. Meanwhile, the tiny version of me on the screen let out a quiet, reedy moan, and I closed my eyes. After a few deep breaths, I paused the video to reply to his email.

> You're cruel.

While I waited for his answer, I moved the frozen corn away from me. My testicles were starting to freeze, though I'd probably be icing them on purpose in a few days. Hello, blue balls.

My phone chimed again, and I checked my email. Uncle Zach's reply made my dick get harder, and it suddenly felt like there wasn't enough room in my ribcage for my heart and lungs.

> Yes, I'm cruel, but that's one of the reasons you love me. And the fact that you love that about me makes me love you all the more.
>
> I can't wait to see you Thursday. I'm going to edge you for so fucking long that when you finally empty those poor, sore balls of yours, you'll do it with a scream because it'll feel like dying and being reborn.
>
> Uncle Zach xxx

Dammit, I was going to cry again. I lifted my phone to my lips and kissed his signature, then I went back to the first email he sent to watch the video again.

Four days and we'd be together again.

TEN
THE CONTRACT

I SAT across from my uncle, wishing we were on our way to his place instead of sitting in a shitty little roadside diner. He'd already delayed our reunion by three more days—it had been a real fucking blow when he'd texted me to say he had a few things to work out before he could see me again—so I felt this side trip to the diner was just plain cruel. I wanted to cry.

"Can't we just eat later?" I sounded like a whiny child, but I couldn't help myself. I'd spent the past few days in a near fever of anticipation, and now that we were together again, I was beyond frustrated.

"We have some things to discuss," he said, pulling out a stack of pages from the messenger bag sitting next to him in the booth. "But first, I need you to do something for me." He held up a bright purple toy with a ring on one end of a narrow, curved shaft. On the other end of the toy was an oblong bulb the size of a walnut.

"Um, okay?" I shot a nervous glance at our waitress, but she was busy serving someone a few booths over.

"I want you to go into the bathroom and put this in. Do you know how it works?" Uncle Zach wasn't exactly being subtle. He held the toy aloft, not bothering to lower his voice.

"No?" My face burned, and I quickly looked around again, but no one was paying attention.

"First, you stick your dick and balls through this loop, okay? I suggest balls first, then dick. Then you're going to put the rest up your ass."

I could have melted into the vinyl bench, but at the same time, my dick perked up, deciding that this was, in fact, the best thing ever.

"Okay," I said quietly. "But. Uh. What . . . what if I'm already, uh, hard?" There was no way I would get everything to fit through the loop if I had a boner.

"That's your problem, not mine," Uncle Zach replied, handing the toy over to me along with a single-serve packet of lube.

I quickly hid everything under the table. "Really?"

"Really. Get to it; we don't have all day."

I sighed and stood, tucking the toy beneath the hem of my T-shirt as I walked as calmly as I could to the bathroom.

In the stall, I closed my eyes and took a few deep breaths, trying to get my dick to behave, but after a minute or two, I was still hard as a rock. Not wanting to disobey my uncle, I dropped my drawers anyway and tried to wrestle the toy around my cock. Thankfully, the material had a little give, and after I got everything through—balls first, then dick, as he had suggested—and was lubing the toy up to get it into my ass, someone tried to open the door.

"Occupied!" I shouted, shoving the toy in faster than I had planned. It wasn't that big, but without any prep at all, it was a little rough. "*Huh . . . it's occupied! C'est occupé!*" I closed my eyes and felt the bulb settle deeper inside me—I guessed that the ring around the base of my cock was to keep the toy from getting lost in my ass. The guy at the door let out a loud sigh, so I quickly did up my jeans and exited the stall, glaring at him as I passed. It was only when I was washing my hands that I realized I hadn't flushed the toilet—dude was probably wondering what the fuck I'd been doing in there since I obviously didn't use the toilet. *Sorry, sir, I was just shoving a toy up my ass to make my uncle happy.* I sighed and stared at myself in the mirror. *You're overthinking things. Relax. No one has a clue what Uncle Zach is making you do.*

However, walking back to the booth, I felt like everyone was watching me. Was I walking funny? I kept my head down, purposefully making my stride slow and casual. Meanwhile, I was so aware of the bulb inside me that it felt like it had doubled in size by the time I eased myself back into the booth.

"All good?" Uncle Zach smiled over his coffee cup.

"Yep."

My uncle then pulled something out of his pocket and placed it on the table next to the stack of papers. It looked like a small remote. I frowned at it, curious, while he unclipped the stack of papers and spread them out in front of him.

"Ready?" he asked.

"Uh. Sure?"

Uncle Zach's smile went coy as he slowly lifted a finger and very deliberately touched one of the buttons on the remote. Immediately, the toy in my ass began to vibrate and jiggle.

Uh oh. "Oh fuck," I whispered.

"That okay? You comfortable?"

I swallowed hard. "Um. Yeah?" My voice went embarrassingly high at the end.

"Faster? Slower?"

I let out an almost silent groan as the toy continued to jostle and buzz my prostate. "No. Uh. This is . . . uh. This is okay."

"You sure?" My uncle looked almost predatory in his amusement. "I can give it a little more juice if you like . . ." His finger hovered over the remote.

"No! No. I'm good. I'm great." My dick was getting harder, snaking down the leg of my jeans, and I shifted to give it more room, but in doing so, I managed to move the bulb inside me so that it pressed more directly into my sweet spot. I took a few deep breaths and chuckled. "Oh god. You know I haven't jacked off in like . . . a week."

"Good." Uncle Zach grinned at me, watching me squirm for a

moment, then he cleared his throat, and his expression went serious. "Okay. Onto business." He slid some stapled pages toward me. "I am in serious need of a personal assistant, and Owen, I think you would be perfect for the job. The hours are all over the place, and sometimes I won't know exactly when I need you, so I'll want you at my beck and call, twenty-four hours a day, seven days a week."

I blinked slowly at him, trying to distract my attention from my throbbing boner and the delicious vibrations inside me. "Um. What? You want me to be your beck-and-call boy?"

"Yes. And I know this is a lot to ask, but you'll need to stay with me to do this job. At my house. A live-in personal assistant."

"Holy shit," I exclaimed. "Fuck, are you *serious*?"

"Dead serious." His business-serious expression cracked, and he winked at me.

"Oh god. That's perfect. It's perfect. Yes—*yes*, where do I sign?" I flipped to the last page and held my hand out. "Gimme a pen."

"Hang on. We need to discuss salary. I was thinking of starting you at sixty."

"*What.*" I stared wide-eyed at him.

"No good?" He frowned and took the pages back. Fishing a pen out of his pocket, he focused on me with a pensive expression. "All right. Seventy." Uncle Zach crossed out something on the second page and scrawled *70k* in its place before handing the contract back to me.

"You're going to give me seventy thousand?" I whispered. "A year?"

"For being my PA, yes. Why? Is that not enough?" He held his hand out for the papers.

"No. That's fine. That's more than fine. Shit, I can't even . . ." I shook my head, taking the pen from him. "Jesus."

A subtle smile played at the corners of his mouth, and as I began signing my name, he tapped the remote again, making the toy wiggle and jiggle and vibrate faster inside me. I gasped, forcing myself to finish my signature.

"And the date."

"The date . . ." I closed my eyes for a moment, panting softly. The loop around my dick acted like a cockring, keeping me good and hard. "What's the date?"

Uncle Zach told me, and I carefully wrote it down.

"Now, this isn't just a pretend job so I can have you whenever I want. You'll do real work, trust me. But it's a good excuse for you to live in my house. Your parents won't even question it."

"Uh-huh." I nodded, wincing as my boner throbbed against my thigh. "Oh god."

"Want me to turn it up some more?"

"No. No . . . please."

Uncle Zach laughed, putting the contract away in his bag. "All right. Next order of business. Speaking of family, starting now, we *cannot* attend family functions together. *Ever.*"

"Um. Yeah. Okay. Good idea." I cleared my throat, rocking slowly back and forth in my seat as if that could distract me from my looming orgasm. "I get it."

"For the time being, anyway. We'll revisit the option in a few months if this is still working out between you and me. But for now, I'm afraid we'll be too obvious."

"Yup!" I said, then clenched my jaw for a few seconds, trying not to let a whimper escape. "I agree."

"Is something wrong?" Uncle Zach lifted one eyebrow, his eyes glinting mischievously.

"Oh god." I lowered my voice, leaning forward to stare at him, pleading. "You're going to make me cum in my pants."

"Am I?" He sipped at his coffee. "Hm. That's unfortunate."

I gritted my teeth, clutching hard at the tabletop. "What . . . else?" I rasped, staring at the last set of stapled pages. I was going to blow my load any second now. My ass and dick were pulsating in unison, and *fuck* did it feel good.

"This is, uh . . . a passport application in case you don't have one and a work visa—we'll be travelling to the US for work occasionally—and some insurance stuff to sign so that you can drive my car if you want to, and some banking info I need from you for deposits, and you know . . .

shit like that." He smiled as he toyed with the remote. "Do you want to read through it all? Might help take your mind off your predicament."

"Can . . . can we just . . . go *oh my god*." I couldn't help the moan that burst from me as he made the toy move faster. "Uncle Zach. I'm not joking. I'm going . . . to cum. Oh. Fucking. God." I squeezed my thighs together, breathing hard.

"Excuse me? Yes, could we get the bill?" Uncle Zach called out.

When I looked up at him, his grin was downright sinister, and I knew he was timing it so that I would cum in my pants in front of someone, and there was nothing I could do about it.

I shut my eyes, holding onto the table for dear life as the pressure grew inside me, sitting there at the *very* tipping point of climax as the waitress approached. I tried to steady my breathing, hunching my shoulders up as my hips moved subtly back and forth of their own accord.

"Hey, are you okay?"

I looked up at the waitress and nodded, trying to keep my expression neutral, not wanting to freak her out. But I knew my face was beet red, and I probably looked like I was having a stroke.

"He'll be fine in a second, don't worry. This happens to him often."

"Like . . . a condition?" the young woman asked.

"Something like that. Owen, you'll be all right?"

My balls suddenly contracted, and deep inside my groin, I felt the rapid muscle flutter signalling my imminent orgasm, and I sat there, face frozen in a contorted rictus as my dick throbbed hard a few times. "I'm *fine*," I said loudly through clenched teeth as the first pulse hit me. I couldn't quite hold back a groan, and the waitress glanced at me, concerned, but I just shook my head, panting as quietly as I could and ducked my head, my eyes clenched tight as I filled my shorts with a week's worth of cum, my ass gaping and clenching down on the bulb with every thick spurt. It was humiliating. I had tears in my eyes by the end of it, but thankfully by that point, Uncle Zach and I were alone again.

"*Fuuuuck*," I breathed. "Oh, Jesus."

"Feel better?" my uncle asked, sitting back in his seat, looking amused.

"No. Yes. I don't know." I rubbed my face with both hands, my ass still twitching around the toy even though he had evidently turned it off.

"You did good."

"Did I?" I laughed then grimaced, shifting in place because I was uncomfortably wet. "Enjoyed yourself?"

"My cock is so hard right now."

"Oh." My cheeks got warm. "Really?"

"*Really*. I wish I could mount you like a bitch on this table right in front of everyone."

I grinned. "Oh yeah?"

"You have no idea. For a second there, watching you struggle, I thought I might need a new pair of shorts too." He stood, tossing a sealed three-pack of boxers on the seat next to me. "Here. Go clean up. I'll meet you in the car."

I got up, tucking the boxers discreetly under my arm. "Thanks. Um. What about the . . . uh, thing? Do I take it out?"

"I plan on wrecking your cunt somewhere on the way home, so it's up to you whether you think your ass can accommodate the toy *and* my dick." He chucked me softly under the chin with his knuckles and winked. "Don't keep me waiting."

I breathed out slowly, watching him go, then realized people *were* staring at me this time. I swallowed, smiling awkwardly, and made a beeline for the restroom.

As SOON AS I got into the car, Uncle Zach started the engine, but to my surprise, instead of pulling out onto the highway, he just drove to the far side of the parking lot and killed the engine.

"Drop your shorts and come here," he said, unzipping his fly. His dick, thick and veiny and soaked with precum, surged out of his pants like a gopher popping out of a hole—he wasn't kidding about being turned on.

I quickly ditched my shorts and straddled him in the driver's seat, carefully avoiding the stick shift. Before I had a chance to settle myself down on my own, he grabbed my hips and rammed his cock up into my lubed hole.

"*Oh*." I clenched my jaw from the abruptness of his thick cock stretching the depths of my ass, but then happily started bouncing in his lap, curling forward so my head wouldn't hit the cloth top as I fucked him.

Uncle Zach groaned and closed his eyes. His tongue came out to skim his bottom lip, so I covered his mouth with mine, sealing us in a slow kiss that stole my breath and made me dizzy.

"Oh god, I missed you," I murmured when I pulled back.

My uncle panted a few quick breaths, his fingers digging into me, then let out a low moan. "Oh, Owen." What I heard in his fierce whisper was beyond want—it was *need*.

My dick was stiffening again, so I started jerking off as I rode my uncle, but then he grabbed me hard by the biceps, holding me down so I was fully impaled on his cock, and opened his eyes with a gasp. When I felt his dick throb inside me, drumming against my prostate, I realized he was cumming. He moaned softly again, his brow deeply furrowed and eyes locked on mine as he emptied himself into me, and I whimpered, sharing in his pleasure as if it were my own. In the intensity of his gaze, I could see meaning: *You are mine*. I was so in love with him, I could barely breathe . . . it was almost scary.

I let out another hushed cry, wishing Uncle Zach would let me move so I could feel his dick spread the slippery mess of his cum inside me, but then he startled me with a sudden sharp laugh. Shaking his head as he smiled, he narrowed his eyes and slapped my hand away from my dick.

"Uh uh. Put it away, Sport. Don't want you to exhaust yourself before tonight."

I blinked. "What's going on tonight?"

"It's a surprise."

When he refused to elaborate, I climbed off him awkwardly and got back in my seat, careful not to get cum on the leather while I wiggled into my boxers and shorts in the cramped space.

"Shall we?" Uncle Zach asked when I was dressed, flashing me a bright smile. Without waiting for my answer, he pulled out of the parking lot and got onto the service road . . . going in the opposite direction from his place.

"Aren't we going home?" I asked, watching the buildings fly by. "Where are we going?"

"You'll see."

I scowled at his profile, annoyed that he was being so cryptic. I just wanted to go home and have him throw me facedown on his bed, spread my ass cheeks, and—*Shit*. I shifted in place, still uncomfortably, achingly hard. I cleared my throat, trying to distract myself.

"So. Um. When do I move in with you?"

"I was thinking this coming weekend. Do you need a truck?"

"Well, that depends. Am I staying in your room?"

"You mean *our* room." He glanced over at me. "Unless you need your own space?"

Our room. My stomach had gone all fluttery with excitement, which apparently was reflected in my expression because he chuckled, reaching over to squeeze my knee before he turned his eyes to the road again. "I take that as a no, then."

"Yeah, no. I'm good with that. And that means I don't need a truck to move my bed. I'll just leave it there. And my dresser. All I have is books and clothes and my computer."

Uncle Zach nodded. "Okay, cool. I'll send some folks from Facilities to pack everything up."

"*What?*" My room wasn't anywhere near the state of Digger's or Jason's—there was just a small pile of dirty laundry at the foot of the bed that I hadn't gotten to yet—but the thought of someone having to touch my grungy boxers was horrifying. "No. I can do it. It's okay."

"Why?" Uncle Zach shot me a teasing glance. "Worried someone is going to see something they shouldn't? Do you have a massive dildo collection under your bed?"

My cheeks reddened. "No." I turned away from him. "I told you —I don't have toys. It's just . . . I'd rather pack up my own stuff."

My uncle patted my knee before returning his hand to the stick shift. "All right, Sport. But can *I* come and help you?"

"Yeah, that's fine." The quivery feeling in my stomach had come back. It was really happening. *I'm moving in with Uncle Zach.* I was nervous and excited and scared and more than a little worried that he'd change his mind and I would be crushed. I closed my eyes. *Don't think about that. Take a deep breath. He* wants *you to move in.*

"You all right?"

I looked over at him and gave a faint laugh. "Yeah, I'm just excited."

"Is this happening too fast?"

"No! No. It's fine. I think I'll feel better once it's all done."

"Is two months' rent for those boneheads you live with enough? Should I give them more?"

"Nah." I smiled. "They'll be fine. You'll take it out of my salary?"

Uncle Zach shook his head, explaining that covering my rent for a few months while my roommates found a replacement was a valid moving expense at his company.

I frowned when I realized we were pulling off the freeway into a strip mall parking lot. "Hey, where are we going?"

"Here," he said, ducking his head to peer at the sign over the double glass doors. With his hand on the wheel, he pointed up.

In graceful blue letters, the sign read: *Clinique de Hydrothérapie.* Then, in a smaller font below: *consultation en naturopathie et irrigation du côlon.*

"A colon cleansing place?" I stared at him. "But . . . I took care of that. Don't worry."

"Think of it as a full spa treatment for your insides."

"But—"

"Trust me . . . you want your ass to sparkle for what's happening later."

I just sat there for a few seconds, feeling embarrassed but intrigued. I *really* didn't want some woo-woo naturopath pressure-washing my guts. But . . . what the hell did Uncle Zach have planned later that I needed this extra level of cleansing?

"Go on. Get." Uncle Zach leaned over me to open my door. "I'll be back for you in—" he checked his watch "—about forty-five minutes."

"What? You're not coming in?"

My panic was clearly audible because he laughed and pulled me towards him to peck a little kiss on my cheek. "I have some errands to run. You'll be fine, Sport. Now, go. I'll see you in a bit."

ELEVEN
CLEANED OUT

WAITING NERVOUSLY for the colon irrigation technician to arrive, I lay semi-reclined on my back, wearing nothing but my t-shirt and socks, a fluffy blue towel draped over my hips, and my hands clasped over my stomach. The room was dimly lit and smelled of lavender and patchouli, and a few Himalayan salt lamps were strewn about the place. Gentle string music punctuated by birdsong played from a speaker in the ceiling, and in front of me were two big paintings of the lower digestive system, done in a dreamy watercolour style. Okay, it was pretty much what I expected—kooky and new-agey—but I had to admit it was relaxing. I might have even dozed off if the door hadn't opened right then, startling me.

"Hello, Owen. I'm Amanda. I'll be treating you today," the young woman said, holding a clipboard with the sheets I had filled out. "How are you feeling?"

I felt weird lying there while she talked to me, so I sat up. "Pretty good, thanks. You?"

"I'm wonderful, thank you!" Amanda's front teeth were endearingly pronounced in her bright smile. She seemed friendly and genuine, and while that should have put me at ease, it made things more awkward for me. I think I would have preferred someone cold and clinical to wash my ass out for me.

"This is your first time, right?"

"Yep."

"Do you have any questions?"

"Uhhh . . ." I blinked a few times dully, my brain going blank. "Um. Does it hurt?"

"Well, you might feel a little cramping . . ."

I listened to her explain the sensations I was *very* familiar with, nodding and frowning with interest in all the right places. *Does Uncle Zach doubt the thoroughness of my routine? Is that why he dumped me here?*

Realizing Amanda had asked me a question, I cleared my throat. "I'm sorry. Could you repeat that?"

"Would you like to watch the whole procedure? Some of our clients enjoy that. They say it's ah . . . reassuring?"

"Like, you can see"—I lowered my voice—"*stuff* come out?"

Amanda cracked another smile, laughing. "Too weird?"

I made a face, though I really doubted there would be anything to see if I *did* watch—my cleansing routine was *tight*, dammit. "Yeah, no thanks."

"Fair enough. Anything else you want to know before we start?"

"Nope."

Amanda had me lie on my side and adjusted the towel so that she had access to my rear.

"Oh wow," she said.

Alarmed, I glanced over at her. "What? What's wrong?"

"Oh my god, that was so unprofessional of me. I'm so sorry. I just . . . I've never seen a tattoo there before. I shouldn't have said anything. I'm sorry."

Relieved, I put my head back down. I laughed—I'd forgotten about my uncle's initials. "Hey, it's fine. Don't worry about it. It *is* a weird place to get one."

She was silent for a few seconds. "Gosh, it must have hurt."

I chuckled, nodding. "It wasn't fun, that's for sure."

Amanda giggled. I could sense she really wanted to ask me what the letters meant, so I said, "It's the initials of someone who means a lot to me."

"Ah." There was a long pause like she was digesting the information and perhaps coming to some conclusions about me and why I would have initials tattooed next to my asshole, but then she surprised me by cheerfully launching into an explanation about how she was going to insert the "rectal tip" of the hose into me, which might feel a little uncomfortable. Evidently, she hadn't picked up on the fact that I *liked* things inserted into my ass on the regular, so I played along like I wasn't a needy size queen with a well-used hole and grimaced on cue as she inserted something the size of a small butt plug into me. Then, I let out what I figured was an appropriate, polite noise of discomfort someone would make if he had never gotten himself ploughed.

"How's that?" she asked when everything was in place and I was on my back again, the hose snaking out between my legs.

"It's fine." It actually felt pretty nice.

Amanda then fiddled with something, and the machine began to hum.

"Ready?"

"Go for it."

My enthusiasm made her laugh again. I heard the click of a button and a louder hum and exhaled as my rectum was suddenly inundated. The water was a little warmer than what I usually use, but not uncomfortable. Amanda began gently massaging my abdomen with just the tips of her fingers as the pressure grew inside me.

"Still good?" she asked.

"I'm great." I closed my eyes, breathing deeply as the water filled me up, and winced as my insides started to cramp. There was a click, and suddenly, the water reversed course, and I sighed in relief. I looked over at Amanda, who graced me with another of her toothy smiles.

"That feel okay?"

"Yup."

She looked down at the hose poking from beneath the towel, and a little frown wrinkled her forehead.

"Is everything okay?"

"Um. Do you have Irritable Bowel?"

"No. Why?" I asked, alarmed.

"It looks a bit like intestinal mucosal lining. It can slough off with stuff like IBD, Crohn's . . . colitis . . ."

My cheeks got hot, realizing she was watching my uncle's cum being flushed out of me. Had he done it on purpose to breed me right before a colon cleanse? Of *course*, he had.

I cleared my throat. "No. It's not that. It's fine. Trust me."

Amanda turned towards me, a question in her eyes, but my reddened face must have tipped her off because it only took a second for her to figure out what was coming out of me.

"Oh . . . you were with . . . oh. *Okay* then." She blushed, obviously holding back a giggle, which only made my cheeks hotter.

I let out a helpless laugh. "I'm sorry."

She shook her head, laughing with me. "No, I'm sorry. This is totally fine. Totally okay. Just give me a second . . ." Amanda closed her eyes and took a deep breath, then released it slowly, gesturing with her hands like she was trying to centre herself. When she opened her eyes, she looked serene again. "There. Now, Owen, how are you feeling?"

"I'm feeling good, thank you," I replied, trying to match her professionalism.

Amanda nodded, then left my side to fetch a bottle. It was warmed massage oil, which she poured liberally on my belly before kneading my bowels like she was making a loaf of bread. Her veneer cracked again only moments later, and she shook her head as she tried to stifle a giggle.

"I'm sorry. I don't know where my head is at today."

"Don't worry about it." I grimaced as she worked my intestines. I thought again about what my uncle could have planned for later. "Today is just full of surprises."

. . .

THE COLON IRRIGATION lasted less than my usual routine, and in the end, it *did* clean a bunch of stuff out, to my surprise. During the second half of the procedure, Amanda had placed heated volcanic rocks on my tummy to release "adhered matter," as she put it, and the last rinse included a probiotic "implant" that was supposed to do something positive to my insides, whatever that meant. My uncle had paid for all the bells and whistles.

The whole experience was quite nice, and I felt incredibly light by the end.

I WAS in the little attached washroom, ridding myself of the last of the water, when I heard footsteps outside the door. *Shit*. I had neglected to bring my pants with me—they were still on the chair out in the room—and I didn't want to walk out half-naked. Amanda had gotten up close and personal with my ass, yes, but it felt wrong to come out with my dick swinging.

"Sorry," I called out, "can you pass me my pants?"

"Why do you need them?"

I blinked and opened the door a crack. "Oh hey!"

Uncle Zach smiled. "Are you done in there?"

"Yup."

He patted the colonic bed. "C'mon. Up."

I frowned. "Uh . . . why?"

"I want to make sure they did a good job."

I laughed, thinking he was joking, but then he lifted his brows expectantly.

"Oh." I got onto the bed and lay back. Then my uncle instructed me to open my legs and bring my knees up. Furiously blushing, I did as I was told, bringing my knees to either side of my chest and holding them there with my arms while my uncle peered at my pristine hole.

"So? Is it to your liking?"

Uncle Zach straightened and grinned. Without warning, he thrust a finger into me, and I gasped, then closed my eyes as he felt for my prostate. My dick, already half hard just from *seeing* my uncle, snaked up my belly.

"Um. What if someone comes in?"

"What if they do?" Uncle Zach wrapped his hand around my shaft, just holding it tight while he fingered me. "Mm. Nice and squeaky clean."

"Oh god." It wouldn't take much to make me cum, but as soon as I let out a soft moan, my uncle stepped away. I pouted. "You're so mean."

"I thought you were worried about someone walking in." Uncle Zach opened a drawer and pawed through it, searching for something. Then he opened a second drawer, frowning.

"What are you looking for?"

"Ah ha!" He showed me a silver device that looked like a duck's bill. It seemed vaguely familiar.

"What is it?"

Uncle Zach gave a single laugh of surprise. He picked up a tube of surgical lube and applied some to the device as he walked back to the bed.

"You don't know what a speculum is?" He looked incredulous.

"No. Should I? *Hey!*"

Startled by my shout, he pulled the speculum away from my hole. "What's wrong?"

"It's *cold*."

"Oh." Uncle Zach grinned. "Deal with it."

The cold speculum slipped inside me easily, and I shivered, wondering what he would do with it. I felt him fiddle around with it, then I gasped as the speculum started opening my hole. *So that's what it's for?*

Uncle Zach watched my face closely as he continued to widen the metal device in my ass, and from his expression, he was enjoying my little groans of protest immensely.

"Oh fuck." I let go of my knees and grabbed for his hand. "S-stop." It felt like my ass was stretched to its limit.

"Too much?"

"Yeah. Oh my god." Uncle Zach took my hand and led it to my hole. *"Holy shit."* I tried to measure the open space with my fingers. It seemed as if I could fit a pop can in there.

"I'd like to go *just* a little wider." He reached for the speculum again, but I groaned and shook my head, holding his wrist to stop him.

"No, that's enough."

My uncle gave me a stern look as he drew my hand away and placed it back on my knee. "Relax, Owen. I'm not going to hurt you."

Closing my eyes, I let out a slow breath, whimpering as he expanded my hole.

"There. See? You're fine," he said, stroking his hand up the back of my thigh. "Man, that looks amazing."

I lifted my head at the sound of a camera shutter and found him taking pictures of my gaped sphincter with his phone.

"I think I'm going to use this as my lock-screen background."

"Oh god." My cheeks grew hot.

Uncle Zach was silent for a few seconds, then shook his head. *"Fuck,* Owen, you have no idea how bad I want to jerk a load into that stretched-out cunt and then piss directly into your guts," he said in a rough voice. He'd put his phone away and had his cock out, stroking it as he focused on my hole.

I huffed out a short breath. My dick had gone soft but was quickly coming back to life. "So do it, Uncle Zach."

My uncle gave a low growl and stepped closer, and I didn't even realize he'd put his dick into me until he hit my deep sphincter. I jerked and cried out at the sudden intrusion, hands scrabbling to his thighs to keep him from moving. It felt so weird to have him so far up inside me without the warmth of his thick shaft sliding against the walls of my ass. It made me feel like an object, just a fuckhole to use, my ass wide open and vulnerable to his whims. I fucking loved it.

I moaned, my dick and ass throbbing as I dropped my arms to my sides, clutching the edges of the colonic bed and squeezing my eyes shut as his cockhead roughly breached my inner hole again.

Uncle Zach grabbed the backs of my thighs and began rapid-fucking me, bending me over double and leaning his weight into me as he thrust hard.

"Fuck, you're such a gorgeous, willing little slut." His fingers dug into my thighs painfully as he slowed, then stopped. He stood there panting. "God, look at you . . . you're as wet as a bitch in heat." I bit my bottom lip as he trailed his finger through the puddle of precum pooling in the shallow divot below my pecs. He lifted it to his mouth for a taste, and I exhaled, my breath trembling. The inner sphincter stretched around his cockhead gave a little spasm as he pushed into me hard for a few more slow thrusts. Then he stopped again. "You'd do anything for me, wouldn't you?"

I nodded, then grew shy under his intense gaze. "Um. Why did you stop?"

"I gotta save it for tonight." Uncle Zach exhaled hard as he pulled his cock out of my hole, giving my ass a longing look as he zipped up his pants.

Though disappointed, I was starting to get nervous—and excited —about what he had planned. "Are you going to tell me what's happening later?"

"Not a chance, Sport." He grinned, then he shook his head again, using both thumbs to stroke the sensitive skin to either side of my hole. "Jesus. *How* are you so perfect for me?"

"I don't know." I shivered at his touch. "Maybe we fit so well together because we're related. Like . . . genetically, we like the same stuff."

Uncle Zach looked up, his hands still on me. "Maybe." He frowned. "There's . . . *nothing* wrong in this. I mean, I *feel* there's nothing wrong in this . . . *us*. But sometimes, it's like I have to keep telling myself that for it to be true."

"There *is* nothing wrong with us being together. Really."

After giving me a fond smile, my uncle leaned down and kissed me gently where his initials were etched into my skin. "All right. We should get out of here." He playfully tugged my balls. "Let's go."

"Uh. Uncle Zach?"

"Yeah, Sport?"

"Aren't you forgetting something?" I raised my eyebrows at him, touching the speculum that was still in my ass.

My uncle let out a long, exaggerated sigh and shrugged. "Oh, all right. Have it your way." He began loosening the device, and I exhaled in relief as the pressure decreased. "I guess we don't want your ass too sore for *you-know-what* later."

I glared, but all Uncle Zach did was grin.

TWELVE
A CATERED AFFAIR

I FROWNED as I stepped through the front door, startled by the flurry of activity at my uncle's place. Two women and a guy about my age were arranging wine and pint glasses on the kitchen island; they wore black shirts and pants with white bowties like waiters. Nearby, Lior and a woman in a headscarf consulted some papers while standing over two big coolers. In the living room, a bearded guy was putting up those umbrella lamps you see in photoshoots, while a guy in a vintage Montréal Expos cap was tapping away on a laptop, seated crosslegged on the floor. The couches had been pushed to the sides of the room, and the coffee table was nowhere to be seen. Up in one corner was a giant screen hanging from the ceiling playing what looked like a nature documentary about ducks.

"What's all this?" I lifted my brows at a curious padded island in the middle of the living room. It was about waist high and had wings to either side, also padded. I ran my hand over the black leather top. *Weird.* "Um, are you throwing a party?"

Uncle Zach smirked and crossed his arms, leaning against the staircase pillar. "You could call it that, yeah."

That's when I noticed the stirrup loops hanging from the ceiling above the padded bench. My heartbeat doubled as I realized what I was looking at.

"Is this . . . uh. Is this a—" I quickly lowered my voice, stepping closer to my uncle. "Is that thing made for *fucking*?"

"Yep. It's a custom breeding bench," he said cheerfully, obviously not caring if anyone heard. "Nifty, eh?" Uncle Zach walked up to the padded bench. He pointed to a pedal set into its base. "And it's accessible to everyone." To demonstrate, he pushed down on the pedal, and the bench went up. Pushing it up with the toe of his shoe made the thing go back down again . . . like a fucking dentist's chair.

"Oh, my god." I glanced around at all the strangers nervously. "Uncle Zach . . . what's going on? Really."

"Well. We're celebrating."

"Celebrating?"

"Yeah. Celebrating you coming to work for me . . . and celebrating you being *with* me." He drew me towards him by crooking his knuckle under my chin until our lips met in a soft kiss. The butterflies took flight in my belly again, making me even more dizzy.

Uncle Zach pulled back and gave me a sly grin. "I couldn't think of a better way to celebrate than to watch my needy little cumdump have his cunt filled by a roomful of strangers."

I let out an involuntary moan, my knees suddenly weak.

My uncle chuckled, gifting me another gentle kiss. "So . . . does that sound good?"

"Fuck yes." I gave a breathless giggle. I glanced around. "And they're the . . . strangers?"

"Oh. *No*." He looked amused. "That's just staff. Three servers, two camera guys—"

"Cameras?" I blinked up at him.

"Sure."

A man carrying a big box from the SAQ came in through the open door. "Where do you want the wine?" he asked in French.

"Lior?" Uncle Zach called out.

The lanky hippie looked up. "Got it, boss man."

"C'mon. Let's get out of their way and get you showered and dressed."

"Dressed?"

Uncle Zach held up a tiny gift bag and grinned.

"Isn't this the exact opposite of what we're supposed to be doing?" I asked, towelling myself off. "I thought you wanted us to be discreet."

"It's fine. Everyone attending tonight has signed an ironclad NDA. Besides, they're primarily here to watch me fuck my nephew and get a load in themselves. I'm not sure how many of them would like that info getting out."

"Yeah . . . I guess." I frowned. "And . . . the live stream?" Uncle Zach had explained that he was broadcasting the event to anyone who paid a nominal viewing fee. "Are we all going to be wearing masks or something?"

Uncle Zach scoffed. "Nah. That's what my algorithm is for. It'll delete any distinguishing marks. Hell, the online watchers don't even know we're related—they're just tuning in to watch a twink getting gangbanged."

"Oh." I chuckled nervously. "How does that work? It'll pixelate faces?"

"No, it's a little more sophisticated than that. Look."

I sat down on the bed where he had been watching me dry off from my shower and looked at the iPad he held. The video playing on the screen showed the staff downstairs preparing, but there was something really odd about their features. I squinted at the screen. It was like their faces were completely generic. I only recognized Lior by his hair and shirt. He looked nothing like himself.

"That's wild."

"Yeah, that's the algorithm I built. It does that on the fly, basically randomizing facial features to create new composites. It does the same with the audio, stripping out the names I fed it."

I watched Not Lior directing the waitstaff for a few seconds.

"Huh. I thought when you said you worked in AI that it was like . . . the kind that creates artwork or writes stories."

"You mean plagiarism software? No. I run an ethical company."

"Oh."

"This specific algorithm is used for stuff like . . . ah . . . surveillance cameras. Especially city-wide ones. It protects everyone's identities—both from city officials and anyone trying to hack into the feed."

"What's the point of keeping people's identities from the city? Isn't that what the cameras are for? You know, Big Brother?"

Uncle Zach smiled. "The way it works is that an official can review an event to determine *if* a crime was committed. Like . . . a mugging, let's say. If there's enough visual evidence of the crime, the official can then have us at CunningAI decrypt the footage with a court order." He wrinkled his brow. "I don't know if I should feel insulted or disappointed that you don't know this already. Didn't you google me?"

I felt my face flush. "Uh. Only as far as trying to find out if you had a secret boyfriend you weren't telling me about," I confessed. Then I grinned. "Why google if I have the real thing?"

My uncle gave me a mock look of disapproval. "Owen, I would *tell* you if I was with someone. And, if you're going to work for me, you should really know what I do for a living."

Draping my arms around his shoulders, I went up on my knees to straddle his lap, rubbing my stiffening boner against his abs as I looked down at him. "I thought my job was just to keep my hole warmed up and lubed for you, twenty-four, seven?" I kissed his smiling lips, loving how his eyes darkened with lust at my words.

"Hmm . . ." he said, playing with my pucker from behind, his fingertip gently stimulating the sensitive nerve endings. "Now I'm sort of regretting planning all of this for tonight. I wish I had you all to myself right now." Uncle Zach let out a little growl. "Maybe I should cancel."

I gasped. "Hey, no way. You can't promise me a fancy catered breeding party and then take it away."

He chuckled, then kissed me deeply as he teased my hole.

"God, I want to fuck you right now."

I felt the same, but I pulled away from him. "Hey! Patience. Aren't we the main event? What would our guests say if you couldn't perform adequately because you . . . uh, overextended yourself?" I grinned, grabbing his hard dick through his pants with both hands.

Uncle Zach pinched my nipple and let out a dramatic sigh. "Damn it, you're right."

I let go of his cock and picked up my uncle's iPad again, blushing a little from the sight of the deep pink tunnel of my stretched-out hole on his lock screen, and held it in front of his face to unlock it. I watched the preparations going on downstairs with him for a few minutes.

"You know, I'm surprised you didn't hire a DJ," I joked.

Looking sheepish, Uncle Zach gave a one-shouldered shrug. "She should be here any minute, actually."

I laughed. The absurdity of it all was thankfully putting me at ease.

"Hey, man, sorry to interrupt."

Turning around, I saw Lior's head poking above the steps.

"Yeah?" Uncle Zach sat up.

"Dave called. He said he can't make it."

"Ah. Damn. Okay, thanks."

"Was he one of the guests?" I asked.

"Yeah. I invited twenty-five—"

"Holy shit." My record was still sixteen—the night Uncle Zach had first fucked me.

"Yeah, well, twenty RSVPed, but one guy cancelled yesterday, and now, without Dave, we're down to eighteen."

"Counting you?"

"Oh, well, if you count me, we're nineteen."

"And Lior?" I turned back to him, my cheeks warm.

"Oh!" Lior climbed the last few steps and scratched the back of his neck. He'd changed into a plain black shirt and jeans, looking more formal than before, even though his shirt was open to his belly button. "I'm going to be busy making sure things run smooth, but, um, yeah . . . Would you *like* me to join in?"

I just nodded, feeling shy.

"Well then, I'm sure I can swing it, kid." His tanned face stretched into a broad smile, only his bottom teeth visible beneath his thick moustache, and his green eyes so warm and friendly that I felt good about my request. I was also looking forward to that thick Prince Albert inside me again. I got a little shiver of excitement from the thought of it.

"Groovy. Well, I'll get back to it." Lior checked his watch. "They'll be arriving in about fifteen, and that keg won't tap itself."

He disappeared down the stairs, and I turned back to my uncle. He had an odd look on his face.

Uh oh. "Was that wrong? Shit, I didn't mean to ask him if I wasn't supposed to."

"Do you think just because I had Lior fuck you once before, that it's okay for you to offer yourself up to him?"

My stomach clenched. "I'm sorry," I whispered. "I wasn't thinking."

"Obviously. What do you think I meant when I said your hole is *mine*? You no longer get to decide who uses it and who doesn't." There was no emotion in his voice.

"I'm sorry," I repeated. Though horrified that I'd fucked up, part of me was tickled with pride over his desire to possess me so completely. "Are you angry?"

Uncle Zach stared at me in silence, making my pulse sing in my ears as I waited anxiously for his answer, prepared to throw myself at his feet and beg for forgiveness.

"No," he finally answered with a small smile. "It's Lior. You get a pass. But don't do it again."

"Okay. I promise!" I said in a rush, relieved that I hadn't messed things up, though a little disappointed that he hadn't promised some sort of punishment. "My hole is yours. I won't forget."

"Good." Uncle Zach gave me a genuine smile this time to show I was forgiven, then reached for the tiny gift bag. "Now . . . time to get into your party clothes." He pulled something black and lacy from the bag and handed it over.

I turned it over, trying to figure out if he'd just handed me a pair of panties, when I saw there was a decent-sized pouch in the front and straps in the back. It was a black lace jockstrap. I'd never seen anything like it.

"Kinky," I said, channelling Lior.

"There's a fun little store in the Village that sells men's lingerie. That's what I was doing while you were getting your treatment. I thought it would look good on you." He grinned. "Go on . . . put it on."

I put on the jockstrap and peered down at myself, wondering if the lacy thing looked good on me. At my uncle's suggestion, I opened one of the black cabinets along the wall and found a full-length mirror inside the door. I gazed at myself in silence. *Wow.* You could see a faint outline of my dick through the lace in the front, and when I turned around, I liked how the curlicued patterns of the straps looked cupping my cheeks. Uncle Zach approached me as I turned to face the mirror again, and he put his arms around me, burying his face in the crook of my neck to kiss along its length.

"You're perfect," he murmured in my ear as he locked eyes with my reflection, caressing me through the black lace with one hand while the other held my throat. "Absolutely fucking perfect."

I closed my eyes, giving in to his touch.

Then the doorbell rang, and instantly, my pulse started racing. When I looked at my uncle's face in the mirror, it wore the same excited expression as mine.

THIRTEEN
LET'S GET THIS PARTY STARTED

MY UNCLE and I sat on the bed, listening to the chatter downstairs. I'd thought we would go down when the first guest arrived, but Uncle Zach had suggested we wait until there was a crowd before making our entrance.

I was excited and nervous and really fucking horny—my dick kept pushing out the black lace and then softening up, caught in a cycle as my thoughts bounced around. *Is everyone going to show up? How long will it go on? Hm. Twenty guys . . . let's say five minutes each . . . That's at least an hour forty. Oh god, I'm going to be sore. But there's Uncle Zach's miracle cream. Oh my god—I'm going to take twenty loads . . .*

Uncle Zach chuckled, interrupting my thoughts, and I turned to him, blushing when I realized he'd been watching my dick do its little dance.

"Can we go down now?" I asked. "Please? The waiting is killing me."

"So impatient!" Uncle Zach shook his head and tweaked my nipple.

"How do you know all these guys anyway? You part of some kind of kinky club?"

"Mm. Something like that, yeah. It started off as a clothing-optional camping group . . . and then the orgies began."

I laughed. "Lakeside gangbangs? Breeding by campfire light?"

My uncle grinned. "Exactly." He sobered after a moment, his eyes going distant. "Then Ed brought his son . . . started passing him around, you know?" Uncle Zach shook his head. "Things got *wild* after that."

"*Oh*." I licked my lips and swallowed, my dick stiff again.

His eyes regained focus, and he stared hard at me for a moment. I wondered if he was considering bringing me on one of those camping trips when he suddenly smiled wide again, adjusting the visible bulge in his pants as he stood. He held his hand out to me.

"All right. Come on. Let's get this party started."

I took it, then gasped as he pulled me to my feet and held me fast against his chest. One hand was splayed on my lower back possessively, with the other cupped around the back of my neck as he hugged me tight.

"I know I keep saying it, but . . . Thank you, Owen," he murmured.

I could feel his heart beating against my ribcage. "For what?"

He pulled back and stared at me with his dark eyes full of emotion. He didn't have to say anything.

I cracked a smile. "I love you too."

Uncle Zach's cheeks dimpled, and he stole a quick kiss before releasing me.

"All right. Let's go show these lovely perverts how well you take your uncle's fat cock."

Suddenly nervous again, I let out a hoarse giggle, and Uncle Zach's sandy brows met over his nose.

"Owen . . . you know you're in control at all times, right? I know it seems like I'm leading the game, but you're the one calling the shots. Don't *ever* hesitate to use your word." He squeezed my biceps, giving me a tiny shake. "Say it now for me."

I loved how easily he could read me. "Pineapple," I said with a shy smile.

Uncle Zach nodded. "Pineapple." We beamed at each other. "Ready?" he asked.

"Yup." However, something occurred to me as he led me to the staircase, so I held back. "Hang on. Am I allowed to cum?"

Uncle Zach tilted his head. "Do you mean with me or the others?"

"I guess . . . both? I mean, it's bound to happen with you. And it might not happen with anyone else . . . I just want to make sure that it was okay. You know . . . if it did."

He smiled at me and cupped my cheek. "Listen, you can cum as many times as you like, Sport. But, I want you to keep something in mind when you do: when it's all over, and it's just us later, you're going to cum one last time for me." Uncle Zach's grin went sly. "Whether you like it or not."

I swallowed, nodding quickly as I adjusted my boner to sit more comfortably in its lace confines.

"Okay." My voice was faint. "Let's do this."

As we descended, the room downstairs went quiet. All eyes turned towards my uncle and me, prompting my pulse to race again and making me unsteady. Uncle Zach squeezed my hand reassuringly as if he could sense how anxious I was. Or maybe he could hear my heart beating so fast—I know I could barely hear his voice above the rushing in my ears.

"Bobby! Glad you could make it. Mike, you bastard—you look damn good. Been hitting the gym? Hey Marco, nice shirt. Ellis! How was Bali?"

Uncle Zach greeted everyone by name, clapping shoulders and shaking hands as he led me through the crowd. I didn't know what to do with my eyes, so I kept my head down as I walked, blushing furiously because of how hungrily everyone was staring at me. I'd done plenty of open doors and anonymous hookups, but this was *nothing* like that. I was a lamb being led to slaughter . . . just a warm piece of meat with accommodating holes.

If my dick got any harder, it would rip a hole in the delicate black lace.

"Everyone, I'd like to introduce someone very special to me. This is my nephew Owen. Owen, say hello."

"Hi," I said quietly, lifting my head.

Most guys were still dressed, but a few had taken their shirts off. One was down to only his purple jockstrap, his arm around the waist of another guy wearing a suit and tie. I looked around. Old and young, fat and thin, and everyone in between.

"That's his nephew? Jesus, they look like brothers," said someone in a low voice.

I grinned.

"Is that everyone?" Uncle Zach asked, turning to Lior.

"Pretty much. Alain phoned to say he was stuck in traffic and not to wait for him."

"All right." My uncle nudged me towards the breeding bench, then unbuckled his belt. "Get on your belly and show me that hole."

I heard a few chuckles, but it was the collective inhale of excitement that made my cock drip through the lace jock as I climbed up on the soft leather surface and went down on my belly, my knees resting on the padded supports to either side.

"Here you go, kid." Lior grinned, handing me a square black pillow. I thanked him and put my head down on it with my arms linked beneath it, hugging it. All around me, guys were talking about me like I wasn't there.

"That is a *smooth* hole," someone said behind me.

"Would you *look* at that?"

"Hey, can you move a bit? I can't see."

"It's up on the screen."

I blinked and looked up. Sure enough, my ass was up on the huge screen in the corner of the room, my hole as smooth as they said, my pucker ever so slightly open and inviting above the black lace that cupped my balls. I breathed out a shaky breath, watching my uncle's thick, veiny cock approach my pretty pink hole. It looked enormous—an impossible fit—but as the lubed cockhead pressed against me, my ass stretched out to accommodate it. I groaned and squeezed my eyes shut, pushing back into my uncle's dick, prompting him to slide his whole length inside me, straight through to my guts. I cried out as he started fucking me, opening my eyes again to watch as the camera angle shifted so I could watch myself being fucked from below, my uncle's balls slapping my taint with every thrust.

I frowned, thinking that something seemed weird, like something was missing, then realized Uncle Zach's initials were nowhere to be seen. *What the* . . .

Then the camera cut to a side view of my uncle fucking me, and I immediately noticed that the tattoos covering his upper body were also gone. Remembering what Uncle Zach said about his algorithm removing recognizable markings, I looked over my shoulder to assure myself that his tattoos were, in fact, still there before turning back to the screen. It was pretty incredible and *almost* seamless. There was a very slight grey tinge to his skin where the tattoos were, but you'd never notice it if you weren't looking for it.

"God, I love how his pussy grips my dick," Uncle Zach said. "He's got such a hungry hole that just *begs* to be bred."

"So breed him already," someone called out, and the group laughed.

I was so distracted by everything going on that I started to think I wasn't going to cum after all, but then Uncle Zach slowed his thrusts, taking his time as he slammed his big cock into me.

"Oh fuck." I gasped as he grabbed my cheeks in both hands, spreading me open as he drove himself deep. "*Huhhh.*"

"And watch . . . all it'll take is my dick in his cunt to make him cream his panties."

Moaning, I buried my face in the pillow as my uncle's fat cockhead thumped my prostate with every thrust, pushing me relentlessly toward orgasm.

I don't think I could have held back if I tried.

"*Fuck.*" I came hard. My wailing cry echoed softly up on the screen as my hole clenched my uncle's dick, doing precisely what he said I would do by sending a hot, messy load into the front of my lace jock.

Uncle Zach started fucking me faster, forcing my still-throbbing, hypersensitive hole to open wider for his thickening dick, and I sobbed out my breaths, clutching the pillow in both fists as he pummeled my guts. Finally, he grunted, his hands like claws on my backside as he pushed his cum deep into my hole with a half dozen shuddering thrusts. Then, with a growl, he pulled out, and I lifted my head to watch the screen across the room as he shook a few thick drops of cum directly into my gaping asshole. *Wow.*

I realized the room had been quiet the whole time he'd been fucking me because I was startled when a little cheer went up, and they all started talking again. I looked around. Most of the guys had ditched at least their pants, and they stood there, dick in hand, as they watched my uncle lean over me, panting.

"Oh, that was fucking good," he said, kissing along my spine. "You ready for the next one?"

I settled my head back down on the pillow, wiggling my hips. "Bring 'em on."

Uncle Zach laughed and slapped my backside. "Okay, who's next?" he asked. "Oh, and Phil? Start up the broadcast."

FOURTEEN
CUMDUMP

THE NEXT COCK in my ass was much smaller than my uncle's, and the guy lasted barely a minute before sending a load into me. He was followed by the couple I'd noticed earlier, and they made out while they took their turns fucking me.

"How's it going?"

I turned to look at Uncle Zach. He took a sip from the champagne flute he held, resting the other hand on my shoulder as if I wasn't lying there with my hole stretched out around some stranger's cock.

"It's going good." I laughed.

He grinned at me, then leaned down to give me a champagne-flavoured kiss. The man fucking me gasped, then grunted, thrusting faster as he came inside me, his orgasm triggered perhaps by watching my uncle tongue my mouth open.

I moaned softly as Uncle Zach's fingers combed through my hair, pulling it gently, and I shivered with pleasure as we kissed. Then my eyes popped open as someone's tongue slipped into my asshole. Uncle Zach pulled back, his brow furrowed.

"What's wrong?"

"I've never been tongued at both ends before," I replied, laughing. The guy eating my ass paused to chuckle.

My uncle straightened, still stroking my hair as he sipped his champagne, his eyes distant.

"Damn, that looks good," he said, and I realized he was looking at the big screen. I turned and exhaled hard as the camera panned in on my spit-wet asshole. Then my uncle and I watched a thick, bulbous cockhead tease my pucker. *Oh god*. It was surreal how insanely horny it made me, seeing my ass up there on the screen swallowing a big dick while feeling it happen at the same time. And it wasn't only me. My uncle took my hand and led it to his hardening cock.

"Fuck, I could watch your boy pussy take cock all day. *Jesus*. Marco, give it to him *hard*."

We watched Marco pound away at me as I stroked my uncle's thick shaft, and I wondered if he was going to fuck me next, but when Marco finally bred my hole and made way for someone else, my uncle wandered off to chat with one of his friends.

The next guy was very large and very hairy. He grabbed me by the hips.

"You've got a really nice body," he said in a soft voice.

"Thanks." I glanced over my shoulder and smiled. I watched him lift his belly with both hands to rest it on me so his dick could reach my hole.

"This okay?" he asked.

"Yeah. Totally. It feels nice." I wasn't lying. It felt great to have my backside fully enveloped by his heavy, furry mass while his cock slowly worked inside me. However, after a minute or two, the weight pressing me down made me realize I should have gone to the bathroom before we got started.

The large man came to a shuddering stop, panting as his dick twitched inside me, and I was going to call for a break when he pulled out, but my uncle was back at my side, pressing down on my shoulder as I started to rise.

"*Hey*, where do you think you're going?" he asked. "Did you want to get on your back?"

"No, I have to pee."

"Lior, can you grab the bucket?"

"What?" I lifted my head, alarmed. "You're going to make me pee in a *bucket*?"

"Sure. That way, you don't need to go anywhere, and we can keep things moving." He took me by the waist and slid me back a few inches so my ass hung off the end of the bench. Then he pulled down my cum covered jock and helped me get my legs out of it. Now my dick was free, pointing straight down at the floor.

I heard Lior place the bucket beneath me and gasped as a new cock breached my hole a second later. I wasn't even going to be given a break to empty my bladder.

"But . . . I can't pee in front of everyone," I whispered.

"You can and you will." Uncle Zach bent down to give me a quick kiss before leaving me again.

My cheeks were hot as I watched him walk away. He really was going to make me piss in a bucket while being fucked. It was humiliating. I knew I could get out of it by using my safeword, but *should* I? I closed my eyes, wondering how long I could hold it. Not very, I knew, because now all I could think about was my bladder. *Fuck.*

I shifted to watch the big screen again to distract myself. Around the video of me getting nailed by a guy in a fedora were smaller images of what I guessed were people logged into the live stream. Some of them were jerking off, which was hot. Then I noticed two numbers. The first was seven, which was easy to decipher—it was the number of loads I'd taken so far—but I couldn't figure out the other.

"Lior?"

He was instantly at my side. "Yeah, kid? Need something?"

"What's that big number on the screen."

"That's how many people are watching."

I blinked a few times, my heart pounding. "You mean, there's like . . . fifty thousand people watching me *right now*?"

"Yep. Wild, huh?"

"Yeah." I frowned. Fifty thousand people were about to watch me pee in a bucket. I *really* had to go, but how could I, with so many people watching?

The guy inside me came with a raspy moan and pulled out, and the count went to eight on the screen.

I knew I was in trouble when the next guy forced his cock into my hole. He was huge, nearly as big as my uncle, which made it worse for my full bladder. I whimpered and attempted to relieve the pressure by lifting my hips as far as they would go, but it wasn't enough. I was nearing the point of no return. Why wasn't I using my safeword? Was I getting off on my uncle putting me in these situations?

Yes. Yes, I was.

I closed my eyes, let out a slow breath, and relaxed.

My stream hitting the metal bucket was *loud* and rhythmic, like it was being fucked out of me—no one could mistake what was happening. I had a feeling that the camera was probably focused on my dick and the bucket, so I kept my eyes shut, slow tears of humiliation soaking into the pillow. Then the sound of my pissing changed. I looked at the big screen and saw a guy had his mouth open between my dick and the bucket. *Oh my god.* He swallowed, then rose up to take my cock in his mouth, drinking my piss directly from the source while the guy above him kept pounding away at my ass.

My dick got hard almost instantly, meaning my stream was cut off, and the piss-drinker pulled away, looking slightly disappointed. I was disappointed, too, because it had felt terrific to have my cock sucked while being fucked.

"There, that wasn't so bad, was it?" Uncle Zach was once more by my side. I glared at him while he ate an hors d'oeuvre.

"You really get off on embarrassing me, don't you."

"Of course. And you love it."

"Hm."

The doorbell rang then, so my uncle went to answer it. I guessed it was the Alain they'd mentioned earlier. Meanwhile, I took another load and then decided it was time to get on my back. Despite the bench being padded, my knees needed a rest.

Moving gingerly to avoid dripping any of my well-earned cum loads, I flipped onto my back, and Lior pulled down on the stirrups so I could put my ankles through. Then he lifted my head and pushed the pillow underneath, making me comfortable. I watched him quietly, liking this weird, thoughtful man more and more as time passed. He gave me a broad smile, then pulled a jar out of his pocket. It was Uncle Zach's fancy cream.

"Need some?"

I laughed. "Yeah. I'm starting to get sore."

"Want me to do the honours, or do you want to do it yourself."

I stared at him, conflicted. On the one hand, yes, I wanted to feel his fingers inside me. On the other . . . was that even allowed? Would my uncle get angry?

Lior held the cream out with a wry grin as if he could read my mind. "Best to be safe, eh?" He winked.

Nodding, I accepted the jar with a thankful smile. After I rubbed the cream into my tender hole, a guy approached me wearing a strap-on. He lowered the bench a few inches, grinning at me as he squeezed my inner thighs and rubbed the silicone dick over the letters tattooed on my taint.

"I'm not going to be able to put a load in you like the rest of the guys. I hope that's okay," he said.

I shrugged. "That's fine." I liked his smile. I also *really* liked it when his smile faded, and his eyes glazed over with lust as he watched himself penetrate me with his thick, metallic-blue cock.

He began fucking me with slow thrusts, startling me when he cried out, red-cheeked and shuddering after only a few seconds. He didn't pull out, just kept on fucking me until he came a second time. I turned to the big screen as the camera panned between his legs to film the action from below and saw that the dildo he was wearing was shaped like an L, with the other end buried in his front hole, held in place by the harness straps. Obviously, it felt great because the guy came a third time while I watched. I was mesmerized by how sopping wet he was.

He stayed put while he caught his breath and grinned at me again.

"Fucking hot, man."

I'd never been fucked by strangers while on my back before. It was . . . odd. It felt more personal. I couldn't decide if I liked it as much as being on my knees. There was just something so satisfying about getting drilled by a complete stranger who doesn't even see your face. And, of course, that's how I wound up being my uncle's personal fucktoy, wasn't it?

Before the next guy came up, Lior approached with a glass of water and held the straw to my mouth so I didn't have to move. I closed my eyes, blissfully drinking the cold, refreshing water.

"Oh god, thank you," I said, smiling, then froze when I saw who had stepped up to fuck me next.

I couldn't breathe around the tightness in my chest for a few seconds.

"M-Mr. S?" I managed, my voice hoarse. I swallowed, trying not to hyperventilate because I was on my back, legs in the air, with cum dripping slowly out of my sloppy hole in front of my tenth-grade math teacher, Mr. Spanoudakis.

"Hi, Owen." Mr. Spanoudakis smiled down at me, sending my pulse into overdrive. I thought I would pass out when he started unbuttoning his shirt, revealing a furry, muscular chest. I suddenly remembered his first name: Alain.

Mr. Spanoudakis wasn't here by accident. *And* he hadn't cared about missing the beginning of the evening with my uncle and me . . . no, he was here *specifically* to fuck me. I glanced over at my uncle, who was standing nearby with a group of guys, one of them getting his dick sucked by the male waiter. Uncle Zach had obviously been watching me, and when I met his gaze, he lifted his champagne flute toward me with a smile.

I turned back to Mr. Spanoudakis in a daze, wondering two things. Firstly, how the hell did Uncle Zach even know him? And second . . . was my uncle aware of the huge crush I'd had on my teacher? I couldn't count the times I'd jerked off to fantasies about Mr. Spanoudakis. He was *gorgeous* with his thick black hair and smooth, olive skin, his face all chiselled and manly and *fuck* . . . I watched Mr. Spanoudakis pull down his boxers, and I thought I was going to die. His dick was just as big and perfect as I'd imagined it.

"Do you want it?" he asked, stroking himself.

"Yes, please," I whispered, so shocked by what was happening that I could barely believe it was real.

Mr. Spanoudakis took a half-step forward, closing the gap between us and began rubbing his cockhead around the rim of my asshole softly, his head down and eyes focused on what he was doing.

I whimpered, blood racing to my dick as I opened my legs wider, desperate to feel that thick cock fill me up.

"Please. *Please*." I felt my pucker open and contract a few times, like it was trying to suck in his cock on its own.

Mr. Spanoudakis laughed. "You haven't changed. Always impatient." He teased at my opening with the smooth, slippery bulb of his glans. "Always rushing through your assignments."

My frustrated moan was cut short as he finally sank his cock into me, and he let out a low grunt of satisfaction as he rooted himself deep. Then he curled his arms around my thighs and began fucking me with slow, smooth thrusts that forced a dribble of precum out of my dick every time he went deep.

Oh my god. I wanted to close my eyes to concentrate on the glorious feeling of being fucked by Mr. Spanoudakis, but at the same time, I couldn't take my eyes off him. I reached up and shyly touched the dark nipples nearly buried in the swirls of black hair and then pinched them softly at his nod of encouragement.

When Mr. Spanoudakis reached for my dick to stroke me as he fucked me, I let out a reedy little cry because I was already so close to orgasm that his touch nearly finished me.

"Oh, you're so wet," he said, closing his eyes as wrinkles formed between his black brows, his breathing becoming heavier.

I didn't know if he meant my ass or my dick, but his words sent me over the edge—I gasped and bucked up against him, forcing him deeper inside me as the first wave hit, growling between clenched teeth as my hole convulsed around his thick shaft and hot cum splashed down on my belly from the cock trapped in his tight grip.

Mr. Spanoudakis moaned quietly, then grunted, fucking me faster as I came on his cock; then he exhaled hard, grimacing as he pumped his load into me with a few body-jarring thrusts.

Once he was done, he stood there panting, a bead of sweat quivering from the tip of his nose, his dark eyes on mine but unfocused, not really seeing me, while his dick gently slid back and forth in the river of cum that flooded my sensitive, throbbing hole. Then he straightened and wiped his face, raking his dark waves back from his high forehead.

"Having a good time?" Uncle Zach asked Mr. Spanoudakis, holding a small towel and a glass of wine out to him.

Mr. Spanoudakis laughed and nodded, accepting the towel, and wiped my cum off his hands before taking the wine glass. His cock was still inside me, slowly softening, and he squeezed my thigh gently. He gazed down at me for a moment, taking a sip from his glass.

"A great time." Mr. Spanoudakis reached down to grab the base of his dick, and though I wanted to watch it happen on the big screen, I kept my eyes on his face and gasped quietly when he winced and pulled out. He smiled down at me.

"See you around, Owen." Mr. Spanoudakis then walked away.

The whole thing had lasted all of five minutes, maybe less, but they were five minutes I would remember for the rest of my life.

Uncle Zach shook his head and gave me a look of gentle reproach.

"I'm not sure I like the way you look at Alain," he said.

I laughed nervously. "Sorry." Then I let out a quiet grunt as someone else started fucking me. "How do you know Mr. S?"

"We used to date," my uncle replied with a smirk, then he bent over and kissed me quickly before returning to his duties as host.

FIFTEEN
DOUBLE OR NOTHING

THE EVENING WAS STARTING to wind down, which was good because my hole was starting to look like a glazed pink donut. The load count up on the screen was up to twenty-five because of repeat performances, and the viewer count was a whopping 85k, which was *insane*. Only about a third of the guests were still there, and I wondered who had already fucked me and who hadn't. The only one I knew for certain hadn't had a go yet was Lior. He'd been busy ensuring everything was in good order, including kicking out a couple of guys who got a little drunk and started making trouble.

My back was getting sore, and I was thirsty, so I waved Lior over during a lull between loads.

"Can I get some water? And I think I want to change positions . . . if there's anyone left. But um . . . if I sit up, I'm going to make a mess everywhere, I think."

Lior laughed. "Yeah, I can see that." He left my side and returned with water which I gulped down gratefully through the straw he held for me.

"Thanks."

"Hey, uh, so did you still want me to join in?" he asked, pensively stroking down the corners of his thick moustache with his pointer finger and thumb.

I was really sore, but I didn't want to disappoint him if he'd been looking forward to fucking me again. "Sure. Of course!"

"Because I've got an idea how to get you off your back without getting spunk all over the floor."

"Oh yeah?"

Lior just grinned. At some point during the evening, he'd taken his shirt off, so he was naked once his jeans were off, save for his gold chain. I watched as he applied a generous amount of lube to his half-hard, pierced cock before gently pushing it into me.

I closed my eyes, taking a deep breath as his stiffening cock gradually opened me up, then looked up in surprise as he lifted my ankle out of the stirrup.

"Put your legs around me," he said, releasing my other ankle. I did as told, then put my arms over his shoulders as he leaned down to scoop me up. "Here we go." Lior huffed out a breath as he lifted me off the bench and then grunted quietly with the strain of carrying me through the living room. "Jess, honey? Can you throw a tablecloth down here?" Lior jerked his head toward the couch, and one of the female servers ran to the kitchen. Lior grimaced at me as I hung in his arms, my legs tight around his narrow waist with his dick plugging my ass.

"You're heavier than you look."

"Sorry."

Once the tablecloth covered the couch cushions, Lior turned around and carefully sat down with me facing him, straddling his lap. "See? Easy peasy and no mess."

I laughed, adjusting myself so that his cock was seated better inside me, then began to ride him slowly. Uncle Zach returned to the living room, having said goodbye to some of his friends, and saw me and Lior. He sat down on the couch next to us and smiled.

"You know what? I think I know how we should end this evening," he said, his grin getting sly.

"Yeah?" The way he was looking at me was making me nervous.

"Your hole is probably so loose it feels like fucking a bowl of warm pudding at this point."

"*Hey.*" I frowned.

"Lior? How stretched out is his pussy? Do you feel anything at all?"

Lior just laughed and shrugged. Then he said, "It's fine."

"It's *fine*?" I stopped moving to stare down at him in dismay.

"Yeah, that's what I thought. Now, if you're going to get the rest of the guys off, you're really going to have to make more of an effort," said my uncle, shaking his head like he was disappointed in me.

What the hell was his problem? "I'm sorry. I *thought* you wanted me to be a passive fuckhole." The physical and mental exertions of the evening were starting to take their toll. I was getting cranky.

"Oh yes. That's exactly what you are. And, you're going to lean forward and relax . . . and remember to keep breathing. That's really important." He flashed a wide smile. "Now, let's tighten up that boycunt. Brian?"

"What?" I blinked a few times at Uncle Zach as a guy approached, stroking his cock, and it dawned on me what he wanted me to do. "No way. I can't take two dicks."

"Why not? It's my hole, and I say it can."

I just stared at him. Part of me wanted to refuse . . . but this was something I'd always wanted to try. Most of the porn I watched had DP in it. It was an incredible turn-on to imagine myself being stretched open by two massive cocks. But the reality? I was sore as hell, and I was *tired.*

"I don't know. I just . . . can't," I whispered, but I *knew* what my uncle was going to say before he did.

"You *can*, and you *will.*"

Lior's dick was still rock-hard inside me. I guess he was unbothered by my obvious distress. Maybe I didn't like him so much after all, but then he rubbed my back and said, "You know it's up to you, kid."

"Shh," said Uncle Zach. "I want to see if Owen will be a good little cockhole and let us wreck his cunt."

"It's going to hurt." My voice caught in my throat as I said it—I could see in his expression that he *wanted* it to hurt. I let out a few nervous breaths. I could safe-word out of it if I wanted to. He wouldn't hold it against me. I *knew* it. I trusted him. He would back down the *second* I refused for real. I also knew he was egging me on because he really believed this was something I could do, and it was something he obviously wanted to put me through. Lior's dick wasn't huge, and, looking around, I saw only a few guys waiting for their turns, and they weren't that big either.

I met my uncle's gaze again and held it for a few seconds before I sighed and turned away, silently leaning forward to rest against Lior's furry chest with my face buried in the crook of his neck. He tucked his hands under my backside and moved me up and down a few times, fucking his cock into me while I waited in nervous anticipation.

I jumped a little when the second cock touched the rim of my sphincter, and then I squeezed my eyes shut, willing myself to relax.

"Slowly," Uncle Zach murmured.

I whimpered as my hole stretched to accommodate the incoming cock, and then yelped and jerked as the fattest part of the glans breached me, causing the whole cockhead to slip inside me suddenly. Thankfully, the guy stopped there, giving me a second while I shuddered and wailed, holding tight to Lior. I was covered in goosebumps, sweat trickling down my spine as I rode the wave of pain. After a few deep breaths, the throbbing, gut-wrenching ache subsided, so I nodded, tears running down my cheeks.

"All right. Keep going," said my uncle, his eyes narrowed and cheeks ruddy with the pleasure of watching me suffer for him.

Pressing my face hard against Lior's stubbly neck, I wept quietly as the second cock slid deeper with Lior's hands helpfully holding my ass cheeks apart to facilitate things. But, once both cocks were inside me, and the guy behind me started thrusting into me, I realized that it didn't feel that much bigger than my uncle's cock or the speculum he'd used on me earlier. The fear had made things more painful—once I let go of that, things got much easier for me. It wasn't exactly enjoyable, though.

At least not at the beginning.

It didn't take long for the first guy to shoot his load into the tight confines of my ass, creaming my insides and Lior's slowly thrusting cock. Meanwhile, Lior was muttering something under his breath: " . . .Charlie, Delta, Echo, Foxtrot, Golf . . ." It took me a second to realize he was reciting the NATO alphabet over and over again, probably in a bid to make himself last longer. Then I let out a loud groan as another cock breached me, and I lifted my head to watch what was happening on the big screen.

Watching myself being double-fucked and *feeling* it at the same time . . . I was actually getting a semi. There was no way I was going to cum from it, but I hoped Uncle Zach was recording all of this because the thought of rubbing one out later to myself being DP'ed on video? *Oh god.*

The second guy came with a few loud grunts, and a third guy took his place. His cock was on the small side, so I was in no pain. I glanced over and saw a man watching me with his arms crossed over his chest, his dick hanging limp. But, as I began moaning in time to being fucked, the man's cock began stiffening, and I watched as it went from a small wrinkled thing to a thick, hard curve without him even touching it. I panted, shoving myself down and back so I was fully impaled on the cocks fucking me, wanting to put on a show for the man.

I made him get hard. That was me. He got hard from watching a slutty little cock whore take two dicks in his sloppy whore cunt.

I whimpered, bouncing in Lior's lap while the guy behind me started going balls deep with every thrust. *Oh wow.* I was actually getting close. I started moving faster, and Lior let out a moan, his voice rough with lust.

"*Fuck,* I'm gonna cum," I huffed, closing my eyes. It seemed like my ass had learned to cum on penetration alone, thanks to my uncle. It felt like a fucking superpower.

I slowed down and then cried out as my pucker clamped down hard on the cocks moving inside me, my hole throbbing around them with exquisite pulses that came from deep within, blinding me to everything except the bursts of pleasure that had me sobbing as the tiny bit of cum left in my balls dripped down onto Lior's chest. Shuddering, I stopped moving, my ass so tender that I was in agony even as I gasped and wailed through the last of my orgasm.

"*Fuck.*"

Lior's hands gripped my backside harder, and he let out a deep groan, pushing his dick painfully into me as he came, triggering the other guy fucking me to let loose too and flood my hole with a raspy cry.

When I felt the guy behind me start to pull out, I quickly leaned forward again onto Lior, lifting myself onto my knees, pelvis tilted backwards and up to keep the cum from dripping out of me. In the process, I also freed my ass from Lior's dick—as much as I'd been enjoying being double-stuffed in the end, I was relieved it was over. *My poor hole*. Then a sudden hoarse growl surprised me. I turned to the big screen in time to see the guy who'd been watching me step into frame and jerk a thick load directly into my big, messy gape.

Wow.

If my uncle *wasn't* recording this, I'd be seriously bummed.

"All right," Uncle Zach said, standing. "That's a wrap." He clapped his hands once, a charming smile on his handsome face. "I want to thank you all for coming, both in person and online. And, of course . . . thanks for *cumming*." A little chuckle went around the room. "Phil? You can kill the feed." He waited until the guy in the Expos hat gave him a thumbs-up, and the big screen had gone dark. "Now . . . feel free to stay and finish your drinks and keep the party going for a little longer. DJ Fuxxx and the staff are paid up for another hour, so you can relax and have a good time . . . but I think it's time to take my nephew to bed."

After some words of thanks and farewell from the small group that remained, chatter resumed as before, and the waitstaff started picking up discarded glassware as the DJ put on a super mellow track by Calexico. I really didn't mind that the end of the party was a little anticlimactic. I smirked to myself—there had been *plenty* of climaxes.

I shifted my weight from one knee to the other. My back was getting sore from my position, and I was certain Lior wanted to get out from under me. But how could I move without getting cum everywhere? Fortunately, that dilemma was solved a moment later when something cold touched my burning sphincter. I gasped and turned as Uncle Zach pushed a big plug into my ass, sealing everything in.

"*Ow*, fuck."

"Hey, I won't have you dripping all the way up the stairs," my uncle said, laughing. "Lior'll kill me."

Lior chuckled and stretched his wiry arms along the top of the couch as I got off his lap, his limp cock falling into the puddle of cum between his legs as he opened his thighs to sit more comfortably, a dreamy look on his face. His eyes crinkled at the corners as he looked up at me, his smile hidden in his moustache. "Thanks for a fun night, kid. That was a blast."

I grinned. "Yeah, it was."

"Hey, boss man—want me to send up a plate for you two? You gotta eat something."

Uncle Zach nodded. "Yeah, in about uh"—he glanced at me—"thirty minutes or so."

"Sure thing."

"Why thirty minutes?" I asked, but my uncle just led me away without answering. I waved goodbye awkwardly to everyone, wondering when Mr. Spanoudakis had left and whether I'd see him again. I really wanted to. Maybe Uncle Zach would let it happen one day. I smiled—and *maybe* with some *serious* hole training, I'd be able to take both of them on at once.

A guy could dream.

SIXTEEN
ONE MORE TIME

GOING up the stairs with a large plug buried in my ass felt really weird, and it was like I had to swivel my hips more to get around the girth of it as I walked. My uncle noticed and laughed, saying that he liked the extra wiggle in my step.

"I could sleep for a hundred years," I said, yawning, walking to the bed. "Why did you tell Lior to bring up food in half an hour? I just wanna crash." I didn't have the energy to wait that long and was just too tired to be hungry anyway.

"Did you forget? I said you were going to cum one last time for me."

I turned to him, frowning. "Oh, there's no way . . ." I held up my hand to stop him from interrupting me. "I know, I know: *you can and you will*. But, I'm telling you, Uncle Zach, I'm not sure it's remotely possible at this point."

"You know I could shock your prostate again to milk you like a farm animal. But . . ." Uncle Zach smiled as he put his arms around my shoulders, then he leaned in for a kiss, biting down gently on my lower lip as he pulled my hips flush to his. His dick was getting hard . . . and amazingly, I felt a tiny bit of stiffening in mine. "Mmm . . . see?" He drew back, laughing softly.

"Hm. Kissing is nice, but I'm not sure how far that's going to get you," I said, then let out a tiny groan as gravity and the tired muscles of my sphincter started working against me. The plug slipped a little, and I clenched my ass to make the thick bulb slide back up inside me. However, it immediately began to fall out again.

"Oh god. I have to get this thing out of me." I squeezed my hole, my muscles quivering with the effort of holding up the heavy plug.

"Not yet." Uncle Zach walked to the cupboards and opened one with shelves. He pulled something out of a plastic wrapper, then turned to me with a smile. In his hands, he held a folded pale-blue papery sheet. I immediately knew what it was because I'd worked at the SPCA two summers back.

"Why do you have puppy training pads?" I asked, though I remembered his words: *do you really think this is the first time Lior's cleaned a boy's piss out of my bed?*

He just shrugged and unfolded the absorbent sheet, placing it in the centre of the bed.

"Come here."

I got onto the bed, but Uncle Zach shook his head when I went to lie down.

"On your knees, thighs apart."

"But . . . the plug is going to fall out," I said, keeping my knees together.

"Yes, it is. But first, you're going to hold it in for as long as you can." He walked to the corner of the room and grabbed a glossy black wooden chair, setting it in front of the bed. Then, he sat down facing me and rested his calf on the knee opposite, one hand slowly stroking his hard cock as he gazed up at me on the bed. "Come on. Legs apart."

Jaw set, I stared at him and slowly inched my knees to either side. Immediately, the plug started to slide out of me, and I winced, clenching my ass to force the plug to rise.

"*Huhh.*" I felt the sweat begin to bead on my upper lip. "I'm going to lose it."

"Here . . . let's make it a challenge. You keep that plug from falling out for, hm, say . . . five minutes, starting right now, and you're off the hook for tonight." He checked his watch, then grinned, tilting his head as he played with the silver bar through his nipple. "But, if it falls out of your sloppy cunt before the five minutes is up, I'm going to make you cum, one way or another."

"But—"

"*And* if you keep arguing . . . I *am* going to shock your prostate to force you to cum." His eyes narrowed. "*Twice.*"

I whimpered as my muscles started failing again. I closed my eyes, concentrating as I squeezed my hole as hard as I could. It was only five minutes, right? I could do five minutes. However, I soon started panting through clenched teeth as I fought to keep the plug inside me.

"How you doing, Sport?" Uncle Zach asked, chuckling as he watched me struggle.

I shook my head, my whole body vibrating from the effort of holding in the plug. My jaw was beginning to hurt from how hard I was gritting my teeth. I groaned and stared at the ceiling, visualizing the ring of muscles contracting. My breath came in shallow gasps, and I kept it high in my chest to minimize any downward push. It was making me light-headed.

"How . . . much . . . longer?" It had to be close to five minutes now.

He checked his watch. "Mm. Four minutes and . . . ten seconds."

"What?" I stared at him in dismay. "Are you fucking seri— Oh *fuck.*" I grunted as I tightened my hole, the plug having nearly slipped out of me. Sweat trickled down my sides and back and between my thighs, making things that much harder for me.

Wait . . . *was* it sweat? Or was I leaking cum?

I let out a little cry, knowing I was fighting a losing battle with gravity. It wasn't that I didn't *want* to cum again; I was just absolutely exhausted, body and mind. On the plus side, the slippery plug bobbing up and down inside me and all my clenching had given me a bit of a boner, so at least my uncle would have something to work with. But would it be enough?

My inner muscles suddenly gave up again; this time, I was too late to catch the plug. It fell to the absorbent pad with a thump and a splash as cum spurted out of my gaping hole.

Uncle Zach stood and started clapping, laughing as I went down on all fours, panting weakly as cum pooled around my knees. My ass kept clenching and releasing of its own accord like it too was gulping air.

"Well, you made it to three minutes. Good effort."

"Thanks," I muttered, lowering myself to my elbows as I rested my sweat-damp forehead on the heels of my hands. I expected Uncle Zach to mount me right away, but when I'd caught my breath, and he still hadn't joined me on the bed, I looked up.

My uncle was attaching something black to his dick—it looked like a flat silicone cock-ring, but one that sat just below the head instead of at the base. He smiled when he saw me watching and pushed his stiff dick down to show me that there was a round bristly black knob about the size of a large blueberry right behind the bulge of his cockhead, no doubt to stimulate my prostate as he fucked me.

"Get on your side," he said, kneeling on the bed.

I went down onto the cum-soaked pad, and Uncle Zach curled behind me, spooning me. I shivered as he kissed my nape and slid a hand down my side. His dick poked at my ass as he adjusted the way he was lying, then, without a word, he slipped his cock inside me.

"Mmm . . . *fuuuuck*," he moaned.

I winced, my tender hole quivering around his thick shaft. "Ow."

Uncle Zach chuckled and bit down gently on my shoulder, then reached around to take hold of my mostly-limp cock.

"Your slutty whore cunt has so much cum in it," he murmured, thrusting slowly. He gave a soft laugh. "I can feel it squirting out of your sloppy pussy every time my dick pushes into you."

My cock surged at his words.

My uncle released me, and I let out a small whimper, but when he grabbed my dick again, I realized that he'd only stopped to collect some cum from the pad to slather on my cock.

Eyelids fluttering, I moaned, moving my hips to rub my cummy dick through his grasp. How could he know that was one of my favourite things to do?

"Watching your hole get filled over and over again tonight was one of the hottest things I've ever seen." He licked the rim of my ear, keeping his cock shallow so that the silicone ball stayed on my prostate, rubbing it in time to his stroking hand.

"Why did you keep walking away, then?" I gasped, pushing back into him as he squeezed my cock hard.

"I had to. I was too turned on. I was just going to spontaneously blow my load from watching you getting bred." Uncle Zach fucked me a little harder, going deep for a few thrusts before returning to rub at my prostate again. "And when you took two dicks like a champ?" He sucked in his breath. "It was fucking gorgeous. Your pussy all stretched out tight around those hard shafts fucking into you at the same time, cum leaking out of you. It was hard to hold back . . . I wanted to take my turn and really open your ass wide."

I whimpered, my balls getting tight as precum drooled out of my dick. I was going to cum, after all. *Amazing*.

However, he stopped moving when he felt me tense, then let go of my dick. He just lay there breathing against my nape.

"Why did you stop?" I asked, my voice hoarse with frustration as the climactic build-up inside me ebbed back.

"Because I feel like drawing it out a bit." Uncle Zach scratched gently down my chest, resting his fingers right above the root of my cock, tickling me. "Don't you?"

"No," I said, swallowing. "Uncle Zach, I'm so tired."

"Well, *I'm* not."

My uncle kept bringing me to the brink of orgasm and stopping, edging me over and over again until I was crying freely.

"Please, Uncle Zach, please . . . no more," I said when he'd stopped short again. I was covered in sweat, hiccuping for breath as tears soaked the sheet beneath my cheek. "You're going to kill me."

"Dramatic much?" he said with a chuckle. "Owen, *I* decide when you've had enough."

I let out a reedy little moan as he started fucking me again, his hand around my aching cock. I knew I was going to have to ice my balls again after all this.

Gasping, I rutted back against him as I felt the pressure mount inside me again, the little nub of silicone prodding and stroking my prostate.

"Oh god. *Please* let me cum, Uncle Zach. Please. *Please.* Oh fuck oh god, please?" My voice was high and raspy from pain and desperation. I had no saliva left in my mouth.

"Oh boy," Lior said, appearing at the top of the stairs carrying a small folding table with plates on it. He set it down next to the bed and stood with his arms crossed, watching us, and then laughed at my wail of frustration when Uncle Zach abruptly pulled out, leaving me panting and miserable. "I do *not* envy you, kid."

I glared at Lior through my tears.

"Uh, boss . . . just wanted to let you know that everyone's gone. Catering is gonna pick up the coolers tomorrow morning, and I'll do a run to the Ecocentre after that with the empties."

"Okay, cool. Thanks for taking care of everything."

"You betcha."

I grunted in pain as Uncle Zach grabbed my dick and pushed his cock back into me.

Lior smiled and shook his head, watching my uncle fuck me for a few moments before turning to go. "Alrighty, have fun, you two," he said. "Hm. Think I'll make some of my protein pancakes tomorrow for breakfast. Sounds like you're going to need them."

Moaning, I watched Lior disappear down the stairs—I was already skirting the edge of climax after only a few gentle thrusts. I gulped my breaths, shaking so hard my teeth were chattering as the pleasure mounted swiftly inside me, praying that this would be the one . . . but Uncle Zach pulled out, leaving me hanging once more.

Weeping, I clutched his hand, trying to force him to touch my dick. I felt like I was going insane.

"I want to cum," I begged, shifting my hips back so that his cockhead touched my pucker, but he just retreated with a laugh.

"I know you do, Sport. I do too." Uncle Zach kissed the back of my neck. "It's just that you're so fucking perfect when you're like this. Your tears make my dick *so* hard." He suddenly pushed himself inside me deep, his pelvis flush with my backside. "I could listen to you cry and beg all night. Maybe I should."

"Oh my god, no, *please*," I said, my voice breaking. "I can't anymore. I *can't*."

Uncle Zach gave a low, evil-sounding chuckle, shifting back to fuck me with shallow thrusts. It didn't take long before I was once again teetering on the brink, my eyes squeezed tight, not daring to hope . . . but then my uncle let out a low growl, suddenly fucking me faster and grunting in time with his thrusts as he came inside me.

I let out an actual scream as I came. It was a brief, jarring orgasm that was more pain than pleasure . . . but the release was *everything*. I lay there afterwards, completely drained and aching, not a thought left in my head and feeling almost delirious with bliss.

"Owen?"

In a daze, I looked up to see my uncle standing by the bed. I hadn't even noticed him pull out or leave. My lids slid closed of their own accord.

"Hey, Sport. Don't fall asleep just yet. You have to shower off."

"No." I shook my head weakly. "I'm sleeping." I could feel myself drifting off already.

"Come on."

"Mm. No. Pineapple."

"*Now* you use your word?"

I fell asleep to my uncle's laughter.

. . .

"What's going on?" I rubbed my face groggily. I was on my back on the bed, and the lights were dimmed. Uncle Zach smiled down at me, wiping my chest with a warm wet washcloth.

"I just couldn't let you sleep like this. What a mess." He laughed.

"Mm. Yeah." I shut my eyes again. "Thanks."

"Hey, are you hungry? Did you want to eat something?"

Instead of answering him, I fell back to sleep.

The next time I awoke, the room was dark. My uncle was curled against my back, his arm around my chest, quietly snoring. Only when I shifted a bit to move the pillow lower did I realize he was inside me.

Huh. I lay there picturing Uncle Zach getting ready for bed: washing his face, brushing his teeth, turning off the lights, crawling under the sheets . . . then jerking off until he was hard enough to penetrate me before falling asleep with his dick snug in my warm hole. It was weirdly comforting. He'd also taken care of me by cleaning me up and, judging from the slightly numb state of my ass, treated me with some of his special balm.

I felt . . . loved.

This is my life now. I sighed happily, thanking whatever force had brought him to my hotel room that night. Because of that "mistake," I was my favourite uncle's fucktoy and cockwarmer . . . *and* personal assistant too, whatever that entailed. I nudged my pelvis back as far as it would go, careful not to dislodge my uncle's cock from its place inside me. I smiled, skimming my fingers softly along Uncle Zach's forearm. I was utterly his—mind, body, heart . . . and hole. I was the luckiest guy alive.

BOOKS BY BEY DECKARD

For an up-to-date list of titles, visit:

https://beydeckard.com/blog/buy-my-books/

Max, the Series

Max

Max, the Sequel

Baal's Heart Series

Caged: Love and Treachery on the High Seas

Sacrificed: Heart Beyond the Spires

Fated: Blood and Redemption

Careened: Winter Solstice in Madierus

F.I.S.T.S

Sarge

Murphy

F.I.S.T.S. Handbook For Individual Survival in Hostile Environments

The Actor's Circle

The Complications of T

The Last Nights of The Frangipani Hotel

The Stonewatchers

Kestrel's Talon

Standalone Books

Uncle Zach

Better the Devil You Know

Exposed

Beauty and His Beast

The Blacksmith's Apprentice

SHORT STORIES

Don't Touch Me (UnCommon Bodies Anthology)

Rakka Surprise (UnCommon Lands Anthology)

ABOUT THE AUTHOR

Artist, Writer, Dog Lover

Bey Deckard is the author of a number of novels including the *Baal's Heart books, Max, Beauty and His Beast,* and *Better the Devil You Know.*

Bey lives in Montréal, Canada where he spends most of his time writing, doing graphic work, painting portraits, speaking French, cooking tasty vegetarian eats, or watching more movies than is good for him. If you're the curious type, www.beydeckard.com is where you'll find art and free stories by Bey as well as information on his published works.

bey.deckard@gmail.com
Look for Deckard's Diablerie on Facebook

facebook.com/authorbeydeckard
twitter.com/BeyDeckard
instagram.com/beydeckard
goodreads.com/beydeckard
bookbub.com/authors/bey-deckard
pettingzoo.co/@Beybey

www.ingramcontent.com/pod-product-compliance
Lightning Source LLC
Chambersburg PA
CBHW011152190726
48288CB00010B/3287